STRANGE HAPPENINGS IN THE HUMAN MIND

Robert Stewart

ISBN: 978-1-8381272-8-2

Friday

PRIOR KNOWLEDGE

She met me with a look of prior knowledge. She had cleared the clutter from her memory and made polite motions to interrupt my attention before I started to realise that she looked familiar. But I was sure that I couldn't put a name to her face. I also didn't know when and where we had met. So, really, I was not confident how exactly the look she had given me might assume anything 'prior' or any kind of 'knowledge'.

She was on one side of the boulevard. I was seated on the other. We were held within the parallel lines of plane trees, which marked one of many routes through the Jardin des Plantes. Joggers weaved around us. A silver-haired man looked over the edge of his newspaper to study his disturbance. A leaf fell.

"Excuse me ..." she said, and hesitated, perhaps because, like me, she was caught in a half-turned memory.

"Oh excuse me," I said, parroting her politeness.

"Yes ... I ...," she hesitated, "excuse me ... I ..."

"Oh ... I ... yes ...," I replied.

Our 'conversation' trudged clumsily onwards.

"You ... ?" she asked, marking out an invisible journey from me to her.

"Yes," I said more confidently, and seizing on the need to make things more intelligible, "Yes ... I recognise ... we have ... have we met before? We have met ... is that what you ...?"

I laughed.

"I recognise you," she confirmed.

"I can't remember your ... sorry ... but, as you say, we have met ... quite recently, I think?"

"I think you must be right."

"Do you remember my ...? ... I'm Alice. I'm sorry this is ... ; I can't believe that I can't remember where we ... but you are so familiar. It was here, wasn't it?"

But immediately I knew that this was not possible. I had arrived in Paris the night before, and, although I had been out drinking, I could remember everything. Discounting the immediate past, the last time I had visited Paris had been ten years ago.

Still, my doubt was only rational. We had met at some point in the space of our shared memory. The fragment of the memory that remained intact also told me that, while we had met in Paris, it was not at this location. Several places came to mind: in particular, a church, a railway station and a bridge. The Jardin des Plantes – the site of our fumbling recollection – did not come to mind.

"I don't know how to say it; ordinarily I would expect the sight of someone to trigger something. But with you ... I recognise you ... but the full memory won't give way."

"I know exactly what you mean," I replied immediately. "I feel the same way."

"It's quite unusual."

She looked determined not to be embarrassed.

"We have to get to the bottom of this."

I agreed.

"What are your thoughts? How do you think we might know each other? I am pretty sure we have never had sex. Wouldn't you say? Not that it rules it out, but I am quite a lot older than you. You must be, what, thirty or thereabouts?"

"Yes, that's right. And, no, we haven't had sex."

"You're English?"

"Yes."

I was English. So was she. We had definitely not had sex. The explanation narrowed.

She had dark hair, in places barely indistinguishable from discreet intrusions of grey. I tried to imagine how my hair might appear in her eyes. It was brown, but with strong and striated lowlights of grey, which, to any critical eye, would signal either a certain state of mind, blatant physiological weakness, or drug abuse. I wondered if, between pondering the problem of where we had met before, she was wondering how I could dye my hair. Perhaps, mentally, she was colouring it ginger in a state of quiet and curious amusement. Or were these just the echo of my own thoughts about a prematurely hoary head?

I had spent the previous night drinking into the early hours. That morning I had woken up just shy of the afternoon, and wandered down from my budget hotel south of the Pigalle. I hadn't felt like doing much, so I had walked until I ran out of fuel in the Jardin des Plantes. She had found me there with my head in a book. This life-lacking 'activity' was non-Parisian: predictable, stuck in a groove, and without the curiosity of three-hundred-and-sixty-degree vision. It made me look cuckolded by my own dry, one-track mind, not mercurial and spontaneous.

I gave the impression that I was studying her.

"Do you live here?" I asked.

She looked a little startled.

"I take it you don't," she replied.

She was slightly stooped in the way she looked at me, and her eyes crouched behind a half-parted curtain of bobbed hair, like the front legs of a spider sticking out of its ancestral crevice. Her eyes were dark, a mixture of brown sugar and black ice.

"Yes, I live here. You're on holiday? Or not?"

"I'm here for the weekend."

"For the weekend?"

She began to see how we might have not met before.

"Yes, just for the weekend."

"Oh," she said, short of any short-term thought.

"Just till Monday," I said. "A long weekend."

"A romantic ... ?"

"... No ... not exactly," I cut her off.

"And you're reading a book," she observed, glancing at my book, "a long weekend in Paris, and you spend it reading a book in the park. That's hardly ..."

"… I know, I suppose I … yes, it's not very …"

"But it's funny, for me, I can understand the reading more than I can understand the … Paris is delightful, of course. I could never deny that. But I just think that … a weekend is not living. It's so … managed and so … neat … and so much like an article written in the travel supplement of a Sunday paper. I mean now that I even think about it in those terms, it makes me want to hate you. Paris is for living. That's not living. But the reading … the reading I can understand."

"Why do you say that?"

She gave me a curious look, one that searched, out of combined hope and indignation, for what I might be. She didn't stop looking at me. There was something measured and restrained despite the swoop of her eagle's flight.

"All I am saying is that if it were left to me, you wouldn't be a tourist. You would be a reader. A park-bench reader. Living – not holidaying – in Paris. And if we have met before, then I would prefer it if you were not what you appear to be."

"Sorry about that," I said.

"Where the hell have I seen you?! I mean for fuck's sake!" she burst out, almost shouting.

She was frustrated with herself, though some of it ricocheted in my direction.

"Yes, it's quite annoying," I said, describing her state of mind rather than mine.

I was curious about where we might have met before, but I was not irritated by my failing memory. So many things had slipped through my mind in the thirty short years I had been alive that it didn't seem either infeasible or confounding that I could have forgotten someone entirely. Birthdays, bills, simple arithmetical processes, a substantial chunk of many films, had all gone missing at one time or another. A sustained experience with another human being was only a modest step up from these hints of brain death.

Sometime soon, I expected that I would reach a state in which I would forget conversations shortly after they had taken place; and, in the absence of a governing sense of time and order, I would repeat the same conversation with one or more people, sailing in a circle of uncharted nonsense. But even the thought of my mind deteriorating in this way, didn't set the alarm ringing. I was stupidly sanguine about the thought of disappearing into a form of mental oblivion in which my only concern was to talk about the weather as many times as I could forget I had already done so.

She reached out and placed her hand squarely on my chest so that she could feel my heart beating. I didn't flinch or recoil. But I don't think I have ever felt so tense. And though her hand had created the tension, it felt like she was feeling for its nucleus in order to temper it.

She stared at me. For a moment, I thought she was on the point of tears. Something stirred in her pupils and it looked like a film of liquid had started to pool.

"There must be a ... a technique for this kind of thing. Don't you think?"

"You mean, memory recall?"

"Yes. People who deal with amnesiacs. They must deal with it all the time."

“Desire perhaps?”

This lit a fire in her mind. She almost shuddered.

“What do you mean?” she asked.

“I mean maybe it depends on how much you want to remember. The more disillusioned you are, the less anchored you must be in anything that would make an experience memorable.”

This time I was describing my state of mind.

“So we have both forgotten for good reason? That’s what you are saying? Bloody hell, that’s gloomy!”

I was still aware that her hand was on my chest, and that I didn’t know why.

I started to laugh. Her interrogation, her hand and her overall manner, felt, if not like psychological torture, then something like psychological tickling.

She smiled.

“No. We will remember,” she said assertively.

SENTIMENTALISM

If she wasn't drunk when I first met her, she certainly got progressively drunk as the afternoon turned to evening and the evening turned to night. Our prolonged encounter was meant to jog our shared memory. Alice said that we should ask each other questions and hope that the answers might sweep away the obstacles that stood in our way. But the answers, often rambling and tangential, were more distracting than anything else. She never even told me her surname. Though she said this didn't really matter because it had changed several times already, and if I waited around for long enough it might change again. So I only know her as Alice.

She made everything else about her personal life sound just as vague. I asked her what she did for a living. She looked indignant, and then said bluntly that this was the sort of pedestrian and unthinking question people asked when they were only looking to make polite conversation.

"Are you only trying to make polite conversation?" she

asked.

"I'm trying to be polite," I replied.

From the Jardin, she had taken me into a café, where she stumbled over the facts of her life. I managed to gather that she taught English. It sounded like she taught at the Sorbonne, but not as a lecturer. I didn't really understand. But this was how she made her living.

"That and alimony," she said.

Most of the time we talked about her. Once or twice she asked me questions but cut my answers short.

"How long are you here for again?"

"Until Monday," I replied.

"Short and sweet."

"I had thought I might stay longer, but work ..."

"Right, I see," she interrupted, and told me an anecdote about an alleged workaholic who really expended his energies on numerous secretaries and office girls.

These exchanges were, I think, meant to be rude, and to make me feel offended. I also sensed that I was supposed to feel guilty about being so stuck-up and morally precious. Obligingly, I managed to fulfil all these expectations, though more because I had intuited them as expectations than because they came to me intuitively.

As far as I could tell, she lived alone in Paris, but with a nexus of friends that sparkled like dew on her autumnal spider web. Even as we drank coffee, two apparent friends approached to pass the time of day. She introduced me, but only as 'un anglais', which sounded distantly insulting.

Until four years ago, she had lived with her daughter,

who had studied for several years at university in London, and was now living in Japan, weeks away from marriage.

"I have only met him once. He seemed nice enough. But you can never really tell. Are you entirely English?" she asked suddenly.

"Yes," I replied. "Why?"

"It's just you don't look completely English. In fact, if I didn't know, I'm not sure where I'd place you."

This question was only a brief aside. She returned to the subject of her daughter as though we had only left it to simmer. She talked at length with unforced and unfettered enthusiasm. She described where her daughter lived, the places she had visited during her time in Japan, many of the friends she had made, and, of course, a closet of well-kept details about her intended son-in-law.

"It wasn't that long ago that I had sushi for the first time," she said, hopping about in an unstructured way under the general heading of Japan. "Imagine that."

I waited on the beat.

"Would you like something to eat? Do you have to be somewhere?"

I told her I didn't. She told me she knew somewhere cheap. And then she ordered a glass of port.

"I often have a glass of port when I have been out in the rain. It isn't raining now, I know. But even so. Port is one of the things I remember from my childhood. My father would give me port when I had a cold. I like the little glasses."

I dared to ask a question.

"How is it you ended up living here?"

"It was something to do with the kind of life I led," she said straight away. "I was a few years younger than you. Twenty five, I think. I worked as a secretary for Kodak. There were a few other secretaries. We were all very different. You know how girls are. But I was ... the only right word is 'dowdy'. I was shy, plain, stiff. I didn't have a boyfriend. My hair seemed to be unmanageable. And my shoulders ... I saw a photograph of myself not so long ago; I had round, heavy set shoulders. They made me look stooped and submissive. I was a sort of physical act of atonement."

Her face was taut with concentration. It gave the impression that she was trying to describe an earlier version of herself objectively and at a distance, as though she were another person.

"And I was broader in the beam in those days."

She thought for a moment as her port arrived. Her eyes flickered.

"There were some people in that place ... they weren't wicked or malevolent. They wouldn't have committed crimes against humanity. Or I don't think they would. But I didn't like them."

"Why?"

"Because I was unhappy, and, at the time, they seemed to play some part in that. I've always found this hard to define, because in some ways it might seem innocuous, and it certainly wasn't direct."

"What wasn't?" I asked.

"I don't know," and she laughed at herself. "No, no, I must

try harder. Let me see if I can explain. Criticism, and sometimes quite cutting criticism, was always implied. No-one would ever say anything openly critical because that wasn't the done thing. So it was always ... ambiguous ... what's the word? ... it was intimated. That's right; it was intimated. And because you knew they were ambiguous and whoever spoke them wasn't speaking their real mind, you never really knew.

'They would say things like 'She's a terribly nice girl but I do find that she expresses herself in rather odd language,' or loudly so that you could just about hear, 'I do think it's terrible when you see someone so far from their natural potential. It's such a shame.' And that old chestnut, 'Of course, no-one is to blame for this, but ...'

'These are silly little observations, I know. But I'm only trying to use them to represent something. There was never any great trauma. No-one ever shouted at me, harassed me or anything like that. But gradually from a quiet but slightly giggly girl, I became this submissive creature who felt she had to apologise for her every move. The word which I always thought was never spoken, but which characterised so much of that job was 'judgement'. To me it seemed like there was some grand personality sitting in judgement over my every move and every word. And I would imagine all the things that people might say about me. All the critical things naturally.

'To me, I inhabited a world in which low self-esteem spread like some silent cancer throughout the body, gradually paralysing all the organs that matter: most of all the brain and the heart.

'In the end I became very angry about it, and, even now, when I look back something tightens in the pit of my stomach, and I feel this self-destructive rage, like I want to commit the most obscene and shocking acts of violence that you wouldn't imagine. It's a sort of apoplectic anger. And now that I look at the mindless, sometimes just plain compulsive, judgements and acerbic language that you find in the press and papers ... I am working myself up. I should stop ...

'I never understood. I could never find the 'right' judgement. I could be wrong, but it seems to me that as soon a small group of Christians invented the idea of putting a man on a pedestal each week and preaching at the community, it became infectious. So that nowadays everyone is a preacher: newspapers, TV, celebrities, politicians, campaigners and political agitators .... But if you take just two – just two, mark you! – of those judgements and you stood them next to each other, they would be contradictory. So who do I listen to? Person one or person two? I still don't understand. Fundamentally I don't understand. But human beings have no respect for naivety. They are unforgiving, and short-sighted. Not like art."

She pointed at me, full of fervour.

"That's why art is better. Because it has respect. It begins from that naivety, and in the process discovers all the things that pompous petty-minded people ruin. I think that's why I get angry when I think about it. Because, of course, I was my own worse victim. I could have gone on being quiet and submissive; I could have remained dowdy and depressed. But in that circumstance, if you want to change things it falls to you, doesn't it? You must stand up for yourself, assert yourself if you are to stand a chance at all. And once you assert yourself, who knows what might happen. In my case you become aggressive and seem to end up treading on the toes of everyone in your immediate vicinity. And then, once they no longer have the energy to contain your unruly behaviour, they try to spirit you away like a headache with pithy little phrases, like 'Oh, not now Alice,' and I always want to say, 'Yes, now! Now for fuck's sake! Always!' ... I'm working myself up. I should stop ... "

She stopped to breathe.

"And then I become angry because I have become angry. Because those instincts of a young and immature girl which were trampled all over by the mysterious formalities of public life are gone forever, and out of necessity, out of pure Machiavellian survival, I have done what I had to and clawed back some kind of human dignity. How that happens could mean anything for any number of different people. In my case, like a lot of other people, it meant moving to Paris. Today it looks like a cliché. Now you would probably do something else. But that assertion of yourself overrides anything that may have come naturally. I sometimes wonder about that. Is there another me that might have been? Something that wasn't a fight against neurasthenia? A kind of parallel me?"

She finished her port and looked thoughtfully at the empty glass.

"I hear people in England today talk about something called 'the knowledge economy'. It's a phrase that makes me want to spit on the floor every time I hear it. Though I'm not quite sure what it means."

She pushed the empty glass across the table in my direction.

"Would you like anything else?" she asked.

"I'll have another coffee."

We ordered again.

"I'm sorry to go on ..." she said, studying me. "I haven't talked about this kind of stuff for a while. I think the last time was in Japan with my daughter (she was a little taken aback!). But I think it's you. I suppose because you are English and that reminds me ... but there's something about you as well ... Do you mind my talking about all this?"

"Not at all."

"You haven't said much, so far."

I didn't want to reply "That's because I can't get a word in edgewise," which was, at least, a plausible and sparring response. In reality, I felt something like relief as she poured out the potted history of her life. If she had wanted me to give a little more to our conversation, I think I might have found that stressful and not too distantly related to the trauma of trying to engage meaningfully with people through a day's work.

Our uneven contributions to speaking and listening – or apparent listening – were exactly the kind of holiday for which I had hoped. As my mind, at a lazy aristocratic distance, toyed with the story she presented to me, I stole decorative delicacies of pleasure by failing to follow everything she said and noting the way that curtains of hair kept sweeping into her eyes. I suddenly saw her as an unusual creature, like an alpaca or a yak, with a shaggy mop of hair fighting against its general sense of curiosity. And, from here, my imagination took flight: I stepped outside the conversation and imagined she was an alpaca and I was a sloth. She was a pushy puff of enthusiasm and interest, and I was happy to take my time over even the simplest activity, such as moving an arm or rolling an eyeball. How would this conversation work, I wondered?

"Ah hah, so you decided to come to Paris, too?" would say the Alpaca. "It's quite different isn't it. Not Latin America, anyway! Far from home; we are far from home! Still, the food's quite digestible, don't you think? Not so chewy."

"I am enjoying ..." the sloth would reply slowly and thoughtfully, "... the root vegetables."

"The cultural barriers can be a problem though, can't they? I mean you can read the guidebook, but that only carries you so far. Yesterday I was queuing for the Rodin museum. I spat in the face of our tour guide. He didn't take it well."

"And ... eating excrement ... is not socially acceptable," would say the sloth with a melancholy air.

"Interesting. Interesting. Have you been to the Rodin museum?"

Before my mind could drift too far, I managed to reply to Alice's observation that I had not said very much.

"No, I, well ... it's interesting to hear you ..."

"Where are you from?" she asked, sounding a little impatient, and hinting that she wanted to bring things back to business.

"Originally? The north."

"I see. I don't really know it very well. I've been to Manchester, and I had a friend from Leeds. But I don't really know it."

"Uh huh."

"You like the north of England?"

"Yes."

"I'm not sure I really have a home, or want one," she replied a little abrasively.

We mulled over our drinks.

"Do you still live there?" she asked.

"No."

"Why did you leave?"

I shrugged.

"Work."

"It's a bitch, isn't it?"

I laughed.

"I have mixed feelings about it."

"I tell you I didn't when I was your age. Everything I have told ... have you ever seen the Alfred Hitchcock film, Rebecca?"

I told her I had.

"I don't know if you remember, there is a scene about halfway through the film where Joan Fontaine is at the height of despair over her marriage, and her sour and manipulative house mistress, Mrs Danvers, opens the window for her. As Joan Fontaine looks out over the ground below, tearful and thinking about suicide, Mrs Danvers whispers in her ear 'You've nothing to stay for. You've nothing to live for really, have you? Look down there. It's easy, isn't it? Why don't you? Why don't you? Go on. Go on. Don't be afraid.' ..."

Alice smiled.

"... Those are the exact words. I haven't seen the film in years, but those are the exact words. That's the scene I really remember. Because I've always thought that scene represents suicide perfectly. Beatrice in the Divine Comedy might be the personification of the l-o-v-e but Mrs Danvers is the personification of suicide. That sense that things are conspiring against you, beyond your control; that a path is being laid out for your own self-destruction, setting things up for a final efficient nudge over the edge."

I was surprised by this confession.

"But if you discover the conspiracy, that's surely something to feel angry about it, isn't it?"

"Yes, I suppose so."

"Thankfully in a film by Alfred Hitchcock backed by David O Selznick the conspiracy is bound to get found out. Thank God for David O Selznick; he brought the world a sentimental approach to making movies."

"And Ingrid Bergman," I added.

"Yes. You see that's what I aspire to. I want my life to be backed by David O Selznick."

"Right."

"Do you understand what I am saying?"

"Yes ... yes, I do."

"I just want to say that I wouldn't have told just any stranger the kind of things that I have been telling you. Particularly what I just said ... about Mrs Danvers."

I had the feeling that while she was being sincere, there was a note of bargaining about this statement. She wanted me to offer something in return.

By now I was thinking, beyond my default politeness, that all of this really was interesting. And I could imagine how Alice might enfold me within the contradictions of her character, if I were not so reserved and incapable of sustaining any conversation beyond a three-minute set of formal pleasantries. From one angle she was crazy. She had not only lost, but self-consciously suppressed, the self-awareness that keep many people in check among the company of strangers. Granted, the nature of our meeting meant that we were only 'strangers' but I knew that I could never behave in the same way, even with someone I knew. Her whole manner, and the forced, even aggressive, way she confessed everything, told me that she was more than just an open personality; she was determined to be an open personality, as though the purpose and plight of her existence were at stake.

Interesting as this was, I was no closer to remembering. Nothing she had told me rang any bells. Something in our conversation should have helped. I now knew a reasonable amount about her. I knew where she lived, her profession, how many times she had been married, a little about her daughter, the circumstances of her move to Paris, that she had a strong, slightly overbearing, manner tempered by an undercurrent of suicidal self-doubt. By rights, not only should I have fully recognised her, I should have offered to part-subsidise her counselling.

The memory lay thickly on my mind but buried from sight. I searched for associations, but only came to dead-ends. I tried to place her in all the obvious places I had visited in the last ten years (including other places I had been on holiday), but to no avail. Besides, part of the memory as I had known from the start, was Paris; and part of the memory told me that we had met much more recently than the last ten years. It made no sense. Her apparent familiarity was so incongruous it felt like I was walking around with someone else's memory trapped inside my head.

"It's a morbid topic I know, but a few years ago I read Durkheim's book about suicide. I think people say it's been discredited now, but there were some things in it that I thought were true. He goes through these rival explanations for rates of suicide, eliminating one after another. In the end he settles on society. On people. Humankind when they are most exposed to other human beings are more likely to become self-destructive. In the figures he shows that human beings are more likely to commit suicide a) in the summer (when the opportunities to mingle are at their greatest) and b) either mid-morning or mid-afternoon (when we are all at our most engaged with the world). Again, I've always felt there's something true in that. And what does that mean? What does it say about people?"

She didn't try to give an answer and neither did I.

THE DOG

A dog was following us. Alice drew my attention to it. She nudged me in the ribs, and whispered "Just stop and turn around slowly." We stopped, turned around slowly to find the dog staring a little forlornly at us, with an occasional, but hopeful, wag of the tail.

Alice said something that sounded harsh and matriarchal to it. Her words, though I didn't understand them, would have certainly sent me packing. But the dog, no doubt toughened by the streets of Paris, had more backbone.

The dog had a white coat with brown freckles and brown ears. I couldn't immediately identify the breed though it looked familiar. Alice said she wasn't entirely sure either, but she thought it might be a Braque du Bourbonnais.

I bent down to tickle it behind its ears.

"What are you doing?" she said, holding me back. "Don't do that. Like it isn't interested in us enough already! Just ignore it. It might go away."

"I have always liked dogs," I said.

"Didn't your parents ever try to scare you about rabies?"

"It's not rabid. You can tell."

"Well anyway. Come along; if we ignore it, it will go away. No dog is that stubborn. And if it doesn't go away I'll kick it up the arse!"

We walked briskly down the street, if nothing else hoping to outrun the dog. I kept looking over my shoulder to see if it had disappeared.

"We haven't shaken it off," I told Alice. "It's still following us."

"Don't look at it. Keep walking. And try to make conversation. It will think ... we need to appear indifferent. You particularly need to appear indifferent. I am indifferent. Harden your heart. You see? Harden your heart! It's just a dog."

It might not have been so surprising if we had been walking down an empty side street, but we were surrounded by people. And the more we ducked and weaved around the hordes of Parisians and tourists, the more it seemed to attract the dog's interest. I began to feel like a spook unable to shake off a tail.

Alice looked reflectively at the dog.

"Damn dog."

Then she shouted – or at least raised her voice – at the dog once again in French.

I found it interesting that she bothered to switch languages, since its French was probably only marginally better than mine. I thought fleetingly about telling the dog to 'Beat it!' or 'Bugger off!', reasoning waywardly that if it spoke French it might feel some sense of national pride, or if it didn't speak French, it might somehow have learned one or two Anglo-Saxon exclamations in its penurious and desultory little life. I even wondered if a quietly kept knowledge of English might account for its penurious and desultory little life.

But I halted my thoughts before my imagination got the better of my judgement, and recalled my judgement from its unsanctioned leave of absence.

"You don't have anything ... dogs have a very acute sense of smell; there's nothing on you that it might be able to smell?"

"Only my musk."

Alice rifled through her own pockets.

"I don't have anything in my pockets either," she said eventually.

"Then I suppose it must be something other than the way we smell ..." I said, a little quizzically.

Something about the overheated atmosphere around her forehead suggested to me that Alice was thinking hard.

"There must be ... you know, a way to approach this. It must be something about us ... and we need to work out what it .... If we are complacent about this, it may keep following us. And we don't want that."

Alice suggested that we temporarily split up; we would take different routes to an agreed rendezvous a short walk away. Without feeling particularly strongly about her suggestion, I agreed to it. We separated. I walked along the Rue de Bercy on my own, and only stopped to look over my shoulder, as I reached the junction with the street that led to our agreed meeting place.

As I stopped, I could feel my heart beat with a sense of anticipation, and a thrill that hoped the dog was following me. I leaned on the corner of a building, and peered. I turned my head and body around. The dog was there, standing loyally, its tongue lying lazily on its mandible. It sat down, waiting for instruction, or perhaps expecting some sort of edible reward. In truth, if I had been carrying an edible reward, now that Alice was safely out of sight, I would have offered it to the dog.

I leaned forward and tickled it behind its ears. The dog closed its mouth and briefly rolled its eyes in pleasure.

I kneeled down before it and it came closer still, so that I could rub it around the neck. It wagged its tail when I did this, and something about this simple chain of cause and effect made me smile. I knew all too well that I was doing something foolish and Alice's attitude was the sensible one. Currying favour with stray dogs was a dangerous game to play, and one that I was sure could only end in tears. But the persistence of the creature intrigued me. Was this normal? I had come across many stray dogs before, but none of them had ever tried to follow me with such conviction. The most I had experienced before this encounter was a few hopeful glances borne out of an almost comically short attention span.

I imagined that a conversation with an average stray dog would run in a circle of repetition free from time, circumstance and sense.

"Hello," I would say to the average stray dog, "nice to meet you."

"I see you are wearing trousers," it would reply.

"Yes, I am wearing trousers," I would confirm.

"It must be very nice to wear trousers. Particularly at this time of year."

"Yes, I suppose they keep you warm."

"I knew someone who wore trousers once."

"Did you?"

"Yes. They looked a lot like you. And they gave me the burnt end of a croissant."

"That was kind."

"Do you have a croissant?"

"No. Sorry."

"I see you're wearing trousers."

"Yes."

"I met someone not so long ago who wore trousers, but he didn't have a croissant."

"Was that me?"

"Possibly. Where's that burnt croissant then?"

But in the case of this dog, I felt sure that the conversation, while it might not have all the accoutrements of common sense and a linear logic, would have more shape and contain something for both of us.

"Sorry to keep following you," it would say apologetically.

"That's all right," I would reply. "I don't mind."

"Only you know how it is. Circumstances are not always propitious."

"Of course," and I would feel duly impressed by the dog's

vocabulary, quickly forming the impression that here was a canine fallen on hard times.

"These streets don't treat you too kindly, you know. And they don't even let you crap where you want these days. Course, I'm sure you have your own problems."

"Well, truth be told, I can't crap wherever I want either."

"What can I say? That's a dirigiste society for you."

And with this pleasant exchange about our mutual predicament we would strike up a long friendship sustained by frequent get-togethers to play fetch in one of the Jardins.

I watched the dog as I stroked it about the ears once more.

"Okay," I said to it, "come on then."

And we walked towards the rendezvous.

The look on Alice's face betrayed her mind in some way, but I was not skilled enough to read its meaning. Part of me thought she was trying to calculate the best way to have me strip-searched.

"Perhaps you just have a curious kind of animal magnetism?" she suggested, as the two of us approached.

I shrugged my shoulders.

Alice fussed and subjected me to unreasonable interrogation for a while, but in the end she decided that we would keep going with the dog in train.

But before we could act on our decision, the dog interrupted. It barked at us.

"Did it just bark at us?" asked Alice.

The dog barked again, affirmatively.

"Well, what does that mean?" she said.

I wasn't clear whether her conversation was with me or the dog.

"I don't … you're a dog. Go away!" she said, a statement which I was sure even the dog thought was rather foolish.

Our indecision was oppressive. Failure to wrap our brains around the paradox of the dog meant that our silence was also oppressive. It was so oppressive that our limbs formed churlish factions independently of our bodies, and wandered about in an ill-disciplined way at the expense of order and ceremony.

"Well …" said Alice eventually, and then stumbled on her journey towards rounded articulation.

We were not the wit and wisdom of humankind at its most glorious and ground-breaking.

The dog barked again, this time, I detected, with a hint of irritation. Then it moved, keeping its eyes fixed on us, to gauge our response. I reacted intuitively by following the dog. It was strange that, even liberated from the formalities of speech and species, I still felt polite obedience to a request. I didn't say it out loud, but my body seemed to be saying "Well, it wants us to follow it, so I suppose we should."

Alice restrained me with one arm.

"What are you doing?" she asked.

"Oh well … I thought that … the dog wants …"

"The dog wants?"

"It seems to want our attention."

"Oh yes? It's got something to say has it? Like what? Some casual thoughts on the legacy of post-structuralism?"

"Well no … I … don't know … it's … it seems quite … it's

uncanny ... that it should ... I mean I realise it's only a ..."

The dog barked again, not, I suspect, intending to complete my sentence for me (though it was no less eloquent).

"Oh be quiet!" said Alice to the dog.

It barked again, this time with a little comeback. My sympathies were increasingly with the dog.

"This is ridiculous," Alice exclaimed.

"Maybe its owner is in danger," I speculated.

"Come off it! This is Paris. Is it going to lead us to someone trapped in a dark room with an overpowering smell of onions?"

"We won't know unless we follow it."

It took a little more wrangling and inflated indignation before we started to move, but eventually we agreed to follow the dog. And the dog led the way with the conviction and authority of a Bonaparte. We could scarcely keep pace with it, but it would look over its shoulder repeatedly to make sure we were still on its tail.

We returned back to the Avenue Ledru-Rollin. It may have been my imagination, but the dog appeared to be moving faster. Perhaps I was also overly sensitive to emotional rejection, but I thought it had stopped glancing around to see if we were still following.

The dog dodged its way around a crowd of Teutonic-looking tourists, and left us to apologise our way through the throng. On the far side, it was no-where to be seen. It had vanished.

"Can you see it?" I asked Alice. "I can't see it."

"What – the dog? Why, where's it gone?"

We stopped in our tracks and surveyed both sides of the street, reviewing from where we had come, and where we might logically be expected to go next. The dog was not visible. Was it hiding? If so, why? Why would it go to such lengths to capture our attention, lead us on a wild goose chase, and then leave us abandoned in the middle of the street? One answer to this question reflected very poorly on our capacity for circumspect judgement.

“I don’t understand,” I said out loud, obviously disappointed about something.

“I have never really liked dogs,” Alice said, a little out of breath. “Well, perhaps that’s going a bit far. I don’t mind them. If I were to keep an animal as a pet, it would be a cat. Probably. Or something unusual, like an armadillo.”

We took a moment to get our bearings before we thought about our next great leap forward. We were standing outside a church.

“American?” asked an accented voice. “Or English? No, you’re English.”

BY A CHURCH

A scruffy-looking man in a donkey jacket, smiling through a roughly hewn beard, was leaning against one of the linden trees, and eating us up with his eyes. His clothes were literally coming apart at the seams. He raised an arm. I saw a huge hole in the armpit of his jacket. But, in spite of this shabby attire and every effort to run his appearance into the ground, he had an unmistakable backbone of composure. This made me think that the two were related. Was he testing his natural elegance by ripping up every cosmetic effort to enhance it?

"What's the matter? Are you lost?" the man asked.

"No; we're not lost," replied Alice.

"No? Or late or something?" You're out of ... well, I suppose it's none of my business, really. I must say, you don't look like you are a mother and son. I could be wrong. Are you lovers?"

"And I suppose that is your business?" replied Alice.

The man shifted his weight from the linden tree and

choked on a cough for a few moments.

"As a matter of fact ... well, it was more a hopeful question, if you see what I mean."

"I don't see what you mean," replied Alice, flexing her talons.

"You have caught me slightly off guard. As you can see, I was paying my respects as a human being," he said, waving towards the entrance to the church.

If anything, Alice looked even more bewildered and disdainful. "What right mind would do that?" her expression seemed to say.

"So I was not at work. But my work is just that. I am a street performer for – how should I say it? ... I am a street performer for romantic couples."

The man was clearly French, and he had the bony, accented profile of an aristocratic Frenchman. His English was crystal clear and his native intonation only faintly detectable. He even spoke with a hint of something cut-glass and plummy. The fact that he looked so shabby and disordered, and that he declared himself a street performer working for small change between glorifying the created order, made me think that, altogether, there was something a little odd about him.

"And so this, you see" continued the man, "is why I was asking if you are lovers."

"Is that right?" said Alice, her jaw falling under the weight of her scepticism.

"**Are** you lovers?" he asked again.

Alice's eyes rehearsed the lighting of a human pyre.

"No," she said.

And then I started to become distracted. Something caught my attention. I looked again at the facade of the church.

"I must admit that, when I first saw you, I thought it was unlikely. But you never know. Stranger things have happened. You might be a rich divorcee who can afford a playboy."

"Impressions can be deceptive."

"It's true; meaning no insult, you don't really look like a rich divorcee. A divorcee perhaps, but not a rich one. And your young companion is a very poor imitation of a male prostitute."

Fair enough, I thought.

The church was definitely familiar. I moved a little, so that my back was facing the street and I could examine its front in more detail. From this angle, the building silhouetted Alice and her barely concealed hostilities. Here, like an unhappy wayfarer lost in the long darkness of a night menaced but illuminated by a flash of lightening, I remembered something. I not only recognised the sight of Alice, but I also recognised Alice outside this church.

"I suppose he must be your son, or something like that?" continued the man.

"Since we are not, as you have noticed, a couple, then I can't really see how we might continue to interest you. Do you have a special act for families too?"

"No, no," replied the man. "I was just being nosy."

"Oh."

"To tell you the truth, my act is quite limited. But I am always looking for a chance to tell my story. It doesn't really matter with whom. Then again, I am not sure you are right for the parts."

The man expressed a painful act of imagination.

"Somehow you both look very out of place. You don't even look like a mother and son. No, the more I reckon it, the more I would never pick the two of you out of a crowd and bring you together. You are very odd."

"**We** are very odd?" cried Alice.

"Yes. Are either of you in love? Have either of you ever been in love?"

"What kind of questions are they?"

Alice asked the question in a way that suggested she was rapidly deciding the street performer was only a 'street performer' and not someone we should waste any further time humouring.

"They are important questions. These days many people expend an awful lot of their energy on many different things – the pursuit of money, their career, a hobby or interest – but they fail to strike one of the basic chords of human purpose."

"Is this part of your act?" asked Alice, sounding genuinely confused.

"I like to think that my act at least gives that kind of harmonious arrangement a chance. Why don't you give it a go? As I have already said, I am a little doubtful that in your case it will work, but we can only try. It's always worth a try, surely."

"Try what? ..." exclaimed Alice becoming even more exasperated, "... who the fuck are you?"

"I have answered that question already. I make my living by putting the magic back into the relationships of Parisian couples. Though, it has to be said, I work mainly for American couples."

I wanted to see what more of my memory (maybe our shared memory) might return through this place, so I fanned the flames of Alice's infernal fury.

"How? What do you do exactly?" I asked.

"Well, now that's a question. All my performances – if that's what we should call them – begin outside churches, even though they graduate to other places. I do sometimes tout my wares outside Notre Dame, but I don't want to give you the impression that couples hire my services for a five-minute romantic thrill. I work with them."

"Work with them?" said Alice, who was now clearly thinking that this man wore his brains inside-out.

"Over the weekend. That's right. They hire me for several days. And on each of these days we work something out. I am not any cheap street performer you can pick up by the banks of the Seine. I offer a very special service. People know about me through word of mouth. One couple from Ohio who hired me many years ago – they since got married – told one of their relatives about me. Two years later that relative came to Paris with his girlfriend to seek me out. You see, my service is known and respected, partly, I suspect, because I operate under the radar of the more conventional tourist itinerary for romancing couples."

"And what do you do over the three days?" I asked.

"I will not say. You can only find out by taking part. The only hint I am ever prepared to give is to say that my clients must be prepared to play along. The assurance I offer is that they only pay me at the end of the weekend, and only if they choose to. They can even walk away from our arrangement at any time they like. So, if they are nervous leaping into the unknown, I always say 'Well, what have you got to lose?'"

"Right," I said.

"So ..." continued the man "... what have you got to lose?"

Alice was eager to put the matter to rest and move on.

"As you said, we are probably not quite right for your 'performance'," she said in a patronising tone, and grabbed my arm as if to say "Come along dear, and don't mind the local idiot."

"You know," said the man hastily, "I have to say – there is something very familiar about you. Have we met before?"

We were both startled.

I noticed that Alice was looking at the church and fighting against a look of surprise. Then she turned to look at me, as though I might be able to offer her an explanation. It was clear to her that I couldn't, but it was clear to us that we both recognised the church.

"Maybe we have everything to gain," I said to Alice, answering the look she had given me.

We had to sweat things out a little more, but from that point, Alice's truculence mellowed and, like me, she gradually became curious to see if this strange Frenchman might be connected to the stirring memories occasioned by the church.

The man – his name was Rémy – said that he would take up no more than an hour on each of the next three days. His idea of 'street performance' seemed to mislead under trade descriptions, since the 'performance' rested mainly with us. He would give us a brief, he said, and help us to devise a 'theatrical scenario' that we would enact. He provided the story and the characters, and we were to pour life into them.

When he first explained all this, my face, beyond my control, must have crumpled into the state of an unwashed pair of underpants left to rot in the washing basket. I could not see how anyone would ever willing submit, much less part with their pay packet, to spend three successive days acting out the fancies of a rough-cut Frenchman in a drafty donkey jacket. What was in it for them?

The man shimmied about once we agreed to play his puppets, bustling around us and ushering us here and there, to fulfil the subtle arrangements of his histrionic composition. In his excitement, he smoothed out the scenario, the protagonists and the circumstances of the scene we were about to begin. The story was set in Paris but many years ago, in the years after the First World War and the Russian revolution. I was to play the part of a melancholy and outcast watchmaker; Alice, in her turn, was a Russian countess who had found asylum in Paris. For her strident opposition to the new regime, Alice's character comes to realise that a revolutionary assassin has taken cover in Paris and is stalking her. So she tries to assume a disguise by courting the affections of the watchmaker and persuading him to marry her. The first scene – the scene the man was now directing us to perform – recreated the first meeting between the countess and the watchmaker.

"I don't suppose this is a true story, then," I said, but Rémy didn't respond.

I thought the conceit was pretty farfetched, all things considered.

Rémy told me to lean against the wall of the church. He walked backwards away from the entrance, so that he could survey my position and stance. Then he told Alice to walk ten metres back along the pavement, turn and, on her return, the scene would begin. Thankfully, the Avenue Ledru-Rollin was pretty quiet.

"Ready?" asked Alice, before she made her way to her starting position.

Something occurred to me.

"Wait a minute," I said to Rémy, "aren't you going to tell us what to say?"

Rémy's eyes glimmered by the light of the city.

"No," he said, "that's up to you."

"You mean we have to improvise?"

"So, are you ready?" asked Alice, unphased.

As Alice walked towards me and, as my heart began to hammer, it struck me that she didn't look much like a Russian countess. I wasn't sure if I looked like a miserable watchmaker, but then I didn't really know how that would look anyway, so I just tried to look miserable, an act that didn't stretch my natural frame of mind beyond endurance.

I saw Alice approach through the corners of my eyes.

Rémy had made it clear to me that I should look like a man down on his luck. I had just lost someone, he told me; a close friend to whom I had been greatly attached. I fixed my eyes on the same spot of ground and let the blood drain from my veins. Alice stopped before me. Even before she said anything, I could tell that she was overacting. Rémy had told her to consider me with forced interest. I couldn't see her face, but in my mind's eye, her 'force' was more like grievous bodily harm.

"I don't really see why you needed to walk all the way over there and back again," I said, not yet in character.

"It helps to set the mood," she whispered. "Just shut up."

Then something unusual happened. Words flowed from the same boarded-up memory with which we had first recognised each other. Our 'performance' went more or less like this:

COUNTESS
I'm sorry to trouble you, but I believe we have met before.

WATCHMAKER
I don't think so.

COUNTESS
But I am quite sure we have.

WATCHMAKER
I don't forget faces.

COUNTESS
You haven't looked at my face.

WATCHMAKER
I saw you from the distance.

COUNTESS
Did you give me your full attention? I really do believe … I just can't recall where I might have … but that's it! Of course! Of course it is. You're Lanier the watchmaker. I came to see you … now when was it? It must have been …

WATCHMAKER
You didn't. I have never seen you before in my life.

COUNTESS
But I really think you must be mistaken. It can only have been …

WATCHMAKER
… believe me, we have never set eyes on each other.

COUNTESS
You are very certain of … I must say that I find you very curt. Manners cost nothing, you know.

WATCHMAKER
Then I must have lost my manners.

COUNTESS
Lost them? I wonder if you ever had any ...

WATCHMAKER
I do not have many friends. The closest of them I have just lost. My manners, you'll excuse me for saying so, appear to have disappeared in the same act of robbery.

COUNTESS
May I ask you something?

WATCHMAKER
Go ahead.

COUNTESS
Is your name Lanier?

WATCHMAKER
I grant you, it is.

COUNTESS
And are you a watchmaker?

WATCHMAKER
Yes.

COUNTESS
Since I know these two facts about you, does it not seem likely that we might have met before?

WATCHMAKER
I am well enough known. But I never forget a face.

COUNTESS
Well I wouldn't ... what happened to your friend?

WATCHMAKER
Disappeared.

COUNTESS
Not dead?

WATCHMAKER
Maybe. This is my concern.

COUNTESS
But shouldn't you do something?

WATCHMAKER
What do you care?

COUNTESS
A cynical question.

WATCHMAKER
You know, these days there's good reason to be suspicious of strangers like you; I could report you, you know.

COUNTESS
Report me!

WATCHMAKER
A stranger presses their advantage in a persistent and harassing way over an unassuming member of the community.

COUNTESS
Well I ... how dare ... no-one has ever spoken ...

WATCHMAKER
... to you like that before? Why? Who are you?

COUNTESS
No, I ... I was only trying to be friendly. I recognised you and I ...

WATCHMAKER
... you saw an opportunity.

COUNTESS
I have made an unfavourable impression. I see that now. I'm sorry.

WATCHMAKER
You've made an impression.

COUNTESS
I feel that ... it's just that ... I suppose I must have wronged you. Please forgive me.

WATCHMAKER
I wouldn't put it that way.

COUNTESS
Will you accept my apologies?

WATCHMAKER
Fine.

COUNTESS
And perhaps ... perhaps, by way of apology, I might help you to find your friend.

WATCHMAKER
I don't think you can offer much help.

COUNTESS
Is your friend a sweetheart? Is that it?

WATCHMAKER
No.

COUNTESS
You are – forgive my candour – you are not married, I believe.

WATCHMAKER
You know all about me, don't you?

COUNTESS
I have noticed some particulars.

WATCHMAKER
Ah hah! So you admit it; you are taking me for a ride. I knew it. I could see it from the first. I know your sort ... what did you think? A little bit of flattery and you could wrap me around your finger? Well, not me! I see through people like you every day!

COUNTESS
It's true, you are a very cynical man. Yes. I can see that. But I will admit it. I do have an ulterior motive. I have seen you many times, always at a distance. This was just a ruse. So I really should apologise. And, not only that, I should be more direct and honest. I suppose all of this – all of our conversation – is just one long way of saying something very simple: I would like to know you better.

Just as inexplicably as Alice and I had known where to begin, we knew that our lines ended at this point. We spoke the dialogue like we had rehearsed it so many times that it would be almost impossible to forget. In the same way that we knew we had met each other before, these lines broke, apparently out of nowhere, into a fluent recreation of a story the outline and details of which I barely knew. As I was speaking, I could not even register my surprise at how I had come to know what I was speaking. The dialogue, like the memory from which it appeared to come, had temporarily overtaken my otherwise undisciplined and vagrant mind.

This was all very extraordinary; and I could tell from the faintly petrified way that Alice returned my gaze, that she thought the same. The most unusual part of the experience was the disarrangement of time. These words were not the recollection of memories we had experienced in the past. They were the memory that had, on impulse, made Alice and I want to greet each other in the Jardin des Plantes. This was clear to me as we spoke our lines. But how was it possible for a memory to come before the events it recalled?

DRUNK

Alice had disappeared. I assumed that she had gone looking for more alcohol. We had found our way to the Marais, and we stared through the single light of a late-night bistro thrown into relief by the deepening night.

Alice had pretty much forced me to eat a bowl of lentils. Then we started on the tequilla. It didn't have that much effect on me, but I kept tempting it all the same. Nearby, two girls in a group of friends, or possibly students, were singing. A shambolic harmony of voices, some cutting in and out as they remembered the words, began to take shape, and then summarily dissolve. By the end of the song, only one of the girls was singing. The group burst into laughter, as they poked fun at each other. I tried to follow what they were saying, but I didn't have the words.

They were all drunk enough to be the wrong side of polite, and in some cases, self-awareness. One of the guys was red in the eye, and disappearing rapidly into a seedy and scratched interior. At best he could manage sometimes articulate phrases or single words. But his drunkenness seemed to make him happy, in a way that without it he might not have been.

Some of them, when they saw that I had been sitting on my own, stole glances at me, and one or two of them were, I could tell, almost tempted to speak to me. If I had been with English people of a similar age behaving in a similar way, I would have wanted to do what I always did as a student: slink away into a corner, until I became so unobtrusive that I could walk home on my own without anyone noticing. Thankfully, I didn't understand a word they were saying.

This thought made me feel cloaked by the language barrier, and, in my mind, protected from the world around me. I felt a sudden rush of comfort. In my retreated position, I looked up out of our lantern of human warmth and animation, at the rooftops of the Marais and, beyond that, into the night.

Paris, I thought suddenly, is a wonderful city. Every legend, myth, cliché, romanticised piece of hokum you hear about it, is true. It is perfectly, seamlessly and unpretentiously at one with its self-image, and happily its image of itself is at one with the image of those looking in on it from the outside. No doubt there are suicides and anxiety, no doubt there is civil unrest, no doubt there is political disaffection and disquiet, no doubt the banlieues offer a very different perspective; but the city preserves itself from implosion of any kind through the perpetuation of its myth. Because the myth works; it hangs around the comical chaos and misdemeanours of human behaviour, like a visible shield that endures. It is not a city of fickle fashion, but an attempt at something more lasting.

Simple things make Paris an attractive place. Haussmann's architecture is one of the most obvious, and it goes to the marrow of the matter. It is a single style; it is one thought in the mind of one man. But it is a good thought. Unlike London, or a few other select historic cities in England which enjoy a kind of architectural and cultural eclecticism, Paris is one idea sustained over time.

And though it has its obvious tourist attractions – the Eiffel Tower, the Louvre, Notre Dame, Le Tours Montparnasse – it is more than the sum of its parts, and there is as much pleasure (if not more) in strolling along the left bank, listening to live jazz in Les Halles, or just staying out late, as there is in following a tightly constructed tourist itinerary. It is a place in which to live (however briefly), rather than observe.

Alice returned eventually. She had persuaded the bar to turn its music on. She then explained that she had been stuck in the toilet for ten minutes, and expressed some concern that I had not bothered to go looking for her ("I might have been drowning in a pool of my own vomit and urine").

She sat down next to me, and placed a bottle of red wine between us.

"For us," she said, "and if you don't drink it, I will."

We had not, so far, said very much about the day's events. Alice had spent much of our meal in a sort of numb silence, concerning herself with small pleasantries and thoughtless gustation. From my early impression of her, I took this to be unusual. She became jokier as she knocked back the tequila, but stayed noticeably off the obvious topic of conversation.

Something about the strange nature of our meeting, and the even stranger scene outside the Avenue Ledru-Rollin evidently bothered her. This was understandable enough. It was, after all, a rude intrusion for any intuitive experience. But, unlike Alice, I was not at all disturbed by what had happened. It seemed completely natural, at least not different from the character and 'feel' of any other memory I could only assemble piecemeal. Looked at logically, I could see that the experience made no sense, but Alice and the words from our piece of street theatre were so ingrained and familiar that they could only feel natural.

So, although I had no explanation for what had happened, it didn't bother me; and even at this stage, my instinct told me that there was, nebulously, something good about the memory we were reliving (or 'living', depending on how you looked at it). I wanted to say as much to Alice, but I didn't know exactly what to say or how to say it. The events were an obstacle to thought, but made me think. In the meantime we just drank.

But the more she drank, the more the alcohol lubricated her willingness to tackle things directly.

"I haven't been to this place for a while. I would expect to see some of my students. That's always a problem," she said. "They would tease me, I am sure. Particularly for being with you. They would say you're my bit of stuff. And I would hear about it in class. 'Who was that young man we saw you with?' they would ask."

"I'm sure they would be reasonable."

She coughed on her laughter.

"But you know," she continued more thoughtfully, "if they were to ask me that question – 'Who was that young man we saw you with?' - the honest answer would be 'I don't know'. Wouldn't it?"

"Well, yes that's true."

"Because I don't know who you are," she reassured herself.

"Uh huh," I grunted.

"And then they would just think I was going mad," she said, this time more philosophically. "A poor old woman who has lost her rag. Too much cheap plonk. Mistreated one too many times by her husbands. She must have left a few too many brain cells behind with '68."

She took a large gulp from her glass of wine, all the while looking consternated.

"Is it just a feature of growing old? Does this happen to you?"

"What?" I asked nervously.

"Where the past looks misguided and ridiculous. No, you're too young, I suppose. I mean there was a time when I felt angry about the proliferation of nuclear weapons," her voice was flattened and distant. "These days I don't. Not because my views have changed, you understand. They haven't. They just seem ... weak. Outpaced by other events. Old. These days there's climate change ... and many other things. But ... I don't know ... I wonder ... "

Her thoughts crashed against her disillusionment.

"I'm not sure I have ever got beyond anything I do looking misguided and ridiculous," I confessed, trying to show some sympathy.

She looked at me directly.

"Do you know me?" she asked directly.

The question came with a lip-smacking taste of self-doubt.

"I ..."

"... No, I don't want you to answer that," she said stopping me before I got started. "You see the way my mind reacts. It wants to turn you into a private dick working for one of my ex-husbands. Someone from the government. Or something like that. But that makes no more sense. Whatever way you try to cut it ... "

"... Yes, I know wh..."

"...You know what I ... you always know what I mean ... you recognise me; I recognise you. We can recite scenes from Casablanca without having a fucking clue about how on earth we ... I'm getting worked up. I should stop."

She took another large draft of wine.

"Why did you come here? To Paris, I mean. Do you mind my asking?"

"I wanted to get away, I suppose."

"Is that all?"

"I suppose."

Alice thought for a moment.

"Do you know why ... ? Well, I have told you already. Do you know why I came here?"

"I think you said."

"Romance. That's why I came."

"Oh that."

She stopped to take this in, and then hiccoughed a little laugh.

I drank as though our conversation depended on it.

"So you thought you would come to Paris?" I said.

"Yeh."

"Right."

"Paris is a romantic sort of place."

She finished her glass and poured another.

"Yes, it's a romantic sort of place."

We waited for something more.

"And you found it."

"What's that?"

"You found romance. When you came here."

"Yes," she said, as though the answer surprised her.

"Congratulations."

I knocked back the wine. She watched me drink.

"And of course, since I last lost it, that means I am looking for it again."

"And how's that going?"

"Well, you know ..."

"Some interest?"

"Some interest, yes. But with me things have a way of never really working out. So my expectations have gradually become more modest. I suppose I must just be a difficult sort of person ... "

"I wouldn't say that."

But, since I could glimpse in her self-description something true, my words felt a lot like a lie.

"No?" she said hopefully, and turned the topic of conversation back to me. "You don't give much away about yourself, do you?"

I shrugged my shoulders.

"I have told you a lot about me, but I hardly know anything about you. Given everything else that has happened, don't you think I should know a bit more?"

"Like what?"

"You tell me."

"There's not much to tell," I said truthfully.

"I don't believe that. I can't believe that. You're, what, thirty?"

"That's right."

"You're part of a hedonistic generation. Your life must be positively shot through with all kinds of bad habits: drug addictions, compulsive sex with strangers, kleptomania ... you know, that sort of thing."

"Not really," I said, a little sadly, "it's pretty uneventful."

"You see – right there; what you said just now; it doesn't give me a lot to go on."

I thought about it for a moment, and I could see no reason to lie.

"Okay. If you really want to know. I work in an office. A government office. Most of my time revolves around work. I don't have many friends. Hardly any in fact. I'm not married. I don't have a girlfriend. I rarely go out. Even more rarely I might speak to my neighbours. I like walking. And reading."

I made my life sound like a flat line of silence. I was, perhaps, exaggerating a little, because I felt strongly that I needed to make it clear to Alice that I did not have compulsive sex with strangers. Strangers might have compulsive sex with each other, but not me. My day-to-day life, to hear my description, began and ended with someone sitting alone in an armchair, sighing as they listened to the melancholy sound of the central heating. Momentarily, I wondered why I was so adamant that Alice should understand my routine of empty repetitions. "I'm an empty vessel," I seemed to be saying, "so why bother?"

Alice thought I had finished, and so did I.

"That's ..." she began, but I felt the impulse to elaborate.

"... but occasionally, I have a week off; or, like now, I come away for the weekend, and things start to seem different."

"How do you mean?"

"I get a sense of ... the possibility of something else."

"Like what exactly?"

Her question betrayed her interest.

"I'm not sure I know exactly what I mean by it, but I want to use the word 'freedom.'"

Alice hadn't moved, but she was practically hugging me. Her eyes sparkled.

"You and I have more in common than I had thought," she said simply.

I smiled at her faintly.

At the end of our 'performance' outside the church, Rémy hadn't said very much. In a business-focused way, that split his mind in different directions, he had said “That was very good”; and then he told us to meet him outside the Gare de Lyons the following day at three o’clock in the afternoon.

“Yes, if you want to keep going, we shall meet then,” he said mysteriously.

Alice and I had felt a little hollow after what had happened outside the church, and so we had not responded. Neither of us had the presence of mind to probe Rémy in the hope that he might broker a sensible explanation; so, with only a few more polite words, he had slipped from our sight and left us dawdling on the street. We had not managed anything like a coherent reflection on our experience by the time Alice said vacantly, “Would you like to get something to eat?”

The cocktail of wine and tequila was swiftly at work in a downwards vortex.

Alice just stared back at me.

“I feel like dancing,” she said.

Saturday

SEX

Not much had changed: the weather was about the same, and I was still hung-over. The only thing that had changed was my position; someone was already sitting on my bench from the day before, so I moved to the one opposite.

We had agreed to meet Rémy later, and I had said I would meet Alice at two thirty in the afternoon outside the Gare de Lyon so that we could prepare ourselves for what might lie ahead and see if, in casting our eyes over the station, it might return more of the extended memory that had, apparently, become the purpose of this long weekend. But this left me with the rest of the day to fill. I acknowledged the thought of more conventional forms of tourism, but quickly decided that I would prefer to revisit the Jardin des Plantes, thinking that by returning to my first glance of Alice yesterday, this might help to shake things into a proper, a more considered and sensible, perspective.

I had walked about the same area in the Jardin, framing the scenery from different angles, in the hope that any one of them might mean something. Try as I did to mentally photograph everything, it made no difference. So, after a time, I slumped into the bench opposite and stared, a little forthrightly, at the unassuming citoyen who had stolen the seat I had called mine only the day before.

It did occur to me that Alice might have the same idea, and that, despite our agreed rendezvous, she might show up in the Jardin; so I was not too surprised when she jumped up on me from behind me. She caught me trying hard not to look at a bottom illiberally 'clothed' by a pair of running shorts. Like the day before, I had been reading for a while, when the distraction appeared.

Through the corner of my eye, a figure jogged into my field of vision. Either she pushed her way out of my peripheral vision and into my clear line of sight, or my clear line of sight went looking for her. She must have been twenty or in her early twenties, wearing lycra jogging shorts that bordered on hot pants, and a skin-tight vest. She was no wiry athlete, but more like a male sexual fantasy taking in some light exercise. She was so full of sex that it made you think your biology was just playing some sort of cruel practical joke.

The person who had stolen the place I had called home only the day before had since moved, and she began to stretch off, using the bench to elasticate her muscles. At first my eyes crept fleetingly off the page. But I was far too self-aware to gawk at her. So I reined in my gaze and fixed it temporarily on the words on the page, scanning vacantly over the lines of typescript. After a short and discreet

– or what I thought of as short and discreet – moment I looked to my left and then, allowing a considered pause, to my right. The garden was fairly quiet, so my eyes strolled casually back to their artificial academic interest, and then pretty much leaped at the object of my poorly dissimulated lust.

I remember once as a student sitting in the university library trying hard to concentrate on a dense piece of text about which I had to write an essay, while a young and very attractive Asian girl sat next to me, her hands clasped together between her legs as she rocked over her own book. I don't think I looked at her once, so perhaps it was a purely imaginary experience, but one that seemed faintly charged with bodies not quite touching. In any case, it made reading difficult. In moments like this, to raise your head and say something (anything) is harder than any study, or act of writing. And I am always convinced that it will end in a cruel and dismissive rejection. So, in my own mind, erotic moments are always intimated and never revealed, they are glimpses stolen by a head that hangs depressively over a ponderous piece of prose.

I could feel the life begin to sink out of my eyes. I was not staring her in the face. I was not taking her out to dinner or to watch a film. I was not engaged in the libidinous game-playing of flirtation and sexual sparring. It was depressing. From my position, it felt like I would always look at this girl like this, and all girls like her in the same way.

Judging by the looks of those that were passing her, I was not the only one thrown into a state of turmoil and discomfort by her presence. I got the impression she enjoyed her lady power. Power, she seemed to say, is something to be enjoyed when it is wielded in the right way.

Slowly, my eyes fell to the ground. I must have looked hollow, drained and defeated.

"She's a pretty girl," said Alice.

I hadn't noticed her creep up on me from behind.

"Do you want to fuck her?"

I looked back at her, partly wanting to say something polite like 'Good afternoon'.

"You don't have to answer. Of course you do. Dear me," she said, objectifying her eyeful, "I think maybe even I do."

She paraded in front of me, pretending to be interested in the plants.

"You get quite a lot of that here," she gestured towards the girl.

"Yes, I can imagine."

"Can you? Really?"

"What do you mean?"

She ignored my question.

"It's strange because judging by the look on your face ... I don't know ... how would you describe it? You certainly didn't look like a young dog about to scamper over to sniff around the bitch on heat. Let's put it that way."

"Crudely you mean."

"Yes. Crudely."

"I suppose you are right."

"So you don't want to fuck her?"

I must have looked uncomfortable.

"Then why the long face?"

"I don't know ... I ... I don't know ..."

"Are you a romantic?"

"Perhaps."

"What if she threw herself at you?"

"I don't know."

"You don't know?"

"I keep my own counsel."

"And how's that working for you?"

"I get by."

"My God, you really do exist behind several layers of permafrost."

"Well ..."

Alice sat down next to me. I looked away from her, perhaps a little distastefully.

"I think you understand me better than you let on."

I looked back to the girl, who was standing with her arms akimbo.

"When I arrived at the Gare du Nord, I stayed on the station. I once had my passport stolen as I walked into the street with a group of other passengers who had just arrived on the same train. Since then I have always tried to put some distance between myself and the batch of new arrivals. So this time I went for a coffee on the concourse ..."

"... and ...?"

The edge had disappeared from her voice.

"I think this is what you want to hear ... or something like it anyway."

"What is?"

"I was sitting down drinking a coffee. A young woman (she must have been mid to late twenties or around my age) sat opposite me, with her child. The child was monkeying around. You know, tugging on her mum's arm, leaning across her knees, generally being a nuisance."

"So?"

"I must have looked … amused. When I looked at the mum, I saw that she was smiling at me. Sort of warmly, as if to say …" I hesitated "… as if to say … 'you know, I can see your heart beating from here'."

A thin flame of excitement shimmered at the back of Alice's eyes.

"You want to be a father?"

"Your offer just now – it's not that … that …"

"What …?"

"I mean isn't there …?"

"… go on …"

"I was going to say, isn't there something about the chase? That's what I have always imagined, anyway."

"What do you mean? Chasing girls?"

"That's right. Courtship."

"Court … look, I know you probably grew up in the age of neoliberalism, but this isn't the 1950s."

"I like 'courtship'."

"Why? It's more traditional?"

"It's politer."

"I don't understand what you are trying to say."

"The word 'courtship' says it all – that there is an implied code of conduct, inside of which you play with each other, tease each other, spar and toy with each other."

" ... I never would have guessed you were like this. Tease each other. I like that."

"I mean there is a game, and through the game you and your character acts out a sort of ritual. You might fail. You might succeed. Both of you know it's only a game, and what it means to play. But the rules of the game are a syntax in which you can at least say something, however fleeting and brief."

"Instead of which ... what?"

"Instead of which you end up fucking strangers in a public toilet high on the latest recreational drug."

"Do you?" she asked, her eyebrows raised.

"Logically speaking. Yes."

"You want rules?"

"I suppose I want meaning. But you can't have that without grammar."

She paused to consider this.

"One part of me thinks you're prudish, another thinks you're just kinky."

I must have looked embarrassed.

"I have to say part of me wishes I were your age," she said.

"And part of me wishes I were yours."

"D'you know at first I thought you were dull ..."

Now it was my turn to be waspish and abrupt.

"But you see what I'm saying – where's the satisfaction in a tryst? That is fucking a stranger in a public toilet high on the latest recreational drug. Where's the achievement, the battle, the sense of adventure – whatever you want to call it – in that? Where's the art, the style, the elegance?"

"So you like a bit of a challenge?"

The girl in the running shorts was on the phone now. She stood with one arm dangling at her side and with the other, she held a mobile to her ear. I tried hard to stay focused on my conversation with Alice and not to look at her; but it was not easy. I found that, in my frequent lapses of will-power, my head unconsciously strayed in her direction, and that when I caught myself doing this, I had to feign interest in a tree, a bird or the ominous approach of clouds. I don't think the girl ever noticed me trying hard to keep my eyes in my sockets, but on reflection she never appeared to acknowledge or notice any of the primitive male interest she provoked. It seemed unrealistic that she could not be aware of this attention, and so I thought that this was part of her presentation to the world: to elicit the attention while keeping her distance from it. Speaking on the phone seemed to suit this attitude. She could stand apart by talking to someone elsewhere, but even as she spoke she was undetectably aware of her body and its radius of influence.

How might she react if someone were to approach her, I wondered? Would this upset the act? Would she be taken aback? Would she treat the person as someone who clearly didn't understand the 'look but don't approach' social etiquette of public running? Or might she welcome the direct attention? Was this the objective? Perhaps she already had a partner, but enjoyed the attention she could still excite.

But how might she react to the approach of someone apparently indifferent to her appearance? Would she mind? I imagined an elderly Norwegian who, as a younger man, had been highly sexed but was now philosophical about it in a laconic Scandinavian way. This Norwegian would be walking around Paris feeling grumpy and he would just want to know a good place to buy some herring. The girl opposite, as she flexed her bottom in public, would be the first person he saw; so he would approach, and, rather testily and in bad French, say "Excuse me, young lady, do you know where I might be able to buy some herring?"

How would she respond? Would her confidence crumble from within? I expected that she would not be too concerned by not winning the affections of elderly Norwegian men with beards that have a permanent smell of herring. So most likely she would just shrug her shoulders and say, "I'm sorry but I don't know," unless, of course, she did.

But, thinking more about this, my imaginary Norwegian gave me some cause for concern. Now that I had brought this figment of my imagination to life and put him to the test of the girl opposite, I found that I envied him in some way. This was alarming. Faced with a girl who appeared to fulfil every particular of male sexual desire, I didn't find myself searching for the looks and charisma that might win her affection; instead I found myself looking for an ageing and misanthropic Scandinavian concerned only with his next supply of North Sea fish.

My fleeting glances at the girl must have mutated through this thought process from repressed sexual desire to sheer confusion.

"I don't know. Maybe," I replied to Alice's question.

Maybe I liked a challenge, but I didn't really know. I had never really had one. A body is not a challenge. It's just a body; even if, like the girl's opposite, it is an appealing one. I felt sure that the near presence of an appealing body and my fantasy of elderly indifference were related somehow, if for no other reason than that neither of them presented the kind of 'challenge' I had tried to describe to Alice.

"I've got to say, it's no wonder you're single; you're a complete freak!" said Alice.

"Yes, I suppose ..."

"Don't say that ... you can't wear it like the Scarlet Letter. I mean, the least you can do is put on a little make-up. Learn a little theatre!"

"What do you mean?"

"I mean ... well, you talked about style and elegance; let's be really shallow for a moment – look at your clothes."

I looked down my front.

"What's wrong with them?"

"That sweater for example."

"What about it?"

"I mean come on, let's face it, you bought it in the supermarket didn't you?"

"So? There's nothing wrong with that. They have some ..."

"Don't come out with all that vapid practical bullshit. Clothes aren't about practicality. I'm talking about style."

"I hadn't thought much ... though I didn't ..."

"What **had** you thought? What **did** you do?"

"I don't ... know ..."

"How much do you earn?"

"What if I mind you asking?"

"I don't care if you mind my asking."

"I do okay. Nothing special."

"Okay isn't a figure."

"I'm not giving you a figure."

"You earn enough to come to Paris for a long weekend. You earn enough to splash out on a sharp suit every once in a while. I mean let's face it, you basically dress like a scientist."

"Are you asking me to go shopping with you?"

"It might be fun, don't you think?"

So we went shopping.

LETTERS TO THE DEAD

Later Rémy showed us several of the letters he had written to his dead English wife. She had died in the 1990s, and her memory, he claimed, had a bearing on the unusual nature of the relationship between me and Alice. Reading these letters, it was obvious that Rémy had planned every word. He would clearly sit down with an idea in his head and a sense of how exactly he wanted to articulate it. There was nothing extemporary or spontaneous about the writing. The fluency and tidiness of the handwriting even suggested to me that he had written everything out more than once, and the final draft was simply an attempt at calligraphy.

One letter read:

My Dear Coumba,

I miss you. Today one of my former colleagues came to visit me for the first time in a long time. He wanted to see how I was getting along. His face – and in particular a sort of worn-thin frown – seemed to say "I'm really sorry I have not been to see you for such a long time, and by the way, it was a truly terrible thing that they did to you. Just awful." Reading his expression, I encouraged him to lighten up. "If there is money to be made from pity – and I am sure there is – I should really try to corner the market," I joked.

He eased up after a while, and we soon returned to talking as though little had changed. I tried to point out to him that I am hardly the object of victimisation and society's indifference to inequity, injustice and exclusion. I have a comfortable pension, and not only that, it is dwarfed by the size of my inheritance. If anything, I am the undeserving rich. In the end we just talked as friends. I discovered that he is due to retire shortly.

That was something I always enjoyed in my professional life: punching through formalities and, finally, talking, one person to another. It's not so often, in such circumstances, that you really see someone's character.

Talking to this friend of mine made me remember all the things that I had enjoyed about my job: the planning, the work involved in making a pitch for something, sitting down in a room, looking at facts, trying to survey the anatomy of a problem and winning respect in the process. I believe he was a little diplomatic in some of the things he told me, but that is no surprise. He smiled grimly when he mentioned certain names. I smiled in return, though I can only guess what exactly he meant me to think.

You can begin to see how my work stimulated me. To sit in a room with intelligent people who have ambitions for their intelligence and insight (such as it is) is exhilarating. But something I noticed, only in passing at the time, is the difference between the way I talked to people through my work, and the privacy of my own thoughts and reflections. At work, the adrenalin and pressure carry you along, and there is something good about this; it knocks you into shape, irons out any indolence and torpor. But it also creates a public language through which it is difficult to recover private space and room for reflection. Many people would find the very idea of private space for reflection an eccentric affectation. I don't agree. At the end of some conferences I attended, I came away feeling enthusiastic, even excited. But in the time I took on my own to think about what I had said, or what had been said, I found myself not so much disagreeing as disillusioned with it.

I remember one occasion in particular; I gave a speech to a congress of international economists on the subject of financial governance. At the time I was pleased with myself. Whether it was the anti-climax that ensued, I don't know, but quickly – within only a few hours or so – I felt deflated, maybe even subdued. Is it enough to find the breath of life through a successful talk on the governance of public finances?

In this frame of mind, I always wanted to fall back on something more concrete, more immediate and personal. I would think about my parents, my childhood, my closest friends. But most of all I would think about you, who I call 'My Dear' or 'My Dearest'. You were the 'most' of my thoughts because you were 'dear' to me (or is it vice versa?). I'm sure we were very close, in ways that, even now, I could not commit to paper.

This difference in form has always interested me: the form of public life versus the form of private life. Each is a mould in which to shape an otherwise unstructured nature. I have not embraced either form with aplomb, and I sometimes think I could have remained in my unstructured nature, a sort of mass of flesh and bone with grotesquely indistinguishable edges, and unable to speak, except perhaps to grunt like an animal. Just think, without you, I might simply have been a blob.

To reassure you that our marriage was, by and large, preferable to the formlessness of indeterminate matter, I was always pleasantly surprised by the shape and form of public and private life. It is a little like eating something you enjoy for the first time: the experience is entirely new, but there is a profound sense of agreement with something basic and needful. I felt the same way when we first had an argument about doing the laundry and you slapped me in the face with a dirty sock.

For all my speculation about unstructured matter, now more than ever, I might become something altogether unstructured. Witness this: I no longer have a job and I no longer have you. I no longer, in other words, have either a public or a private life in which to imprint any kind of form. So I have discovered another form: I write these letters. In your absence they restrain any late illness in my brain.

And in writing these letters, I have found myself pleasantly surprised in a new way. Here, after all, is another un-tasted dish, albeit one that comes from a different culinary tradition. The tastes here are more delicate and understated. This is discreet cooking. It feels to me like a form that is fading. I can no longer see you or sense you in any way, but the words as I write them, as I give them shape, point in your direction; they make you real at one step removed. They are a strange incantation of death-in-abeyance.

I want to make it plain: I really do believe that in writing this – that is in writing the very words 'in writing this' - I am in some sense 'talking' with you once again. The words and sentences are a bridge over a chasm; in them you return to a delicate shape that might shift or dissemble with the slightest provocation, but the shape is one that I can, all the same, begin to sense, like a blind man intuiting the presence of another being close at hand.

Now this must all, of course, seem irrational and call my sanity into question. But 'madness' frames the loss of form that I have made my business. So if there is a hint of madness here, it only signifies creations that must be oblique. There really is method in my madness, or perhaps madness in my method.

When you were alive we would repeatedly run up against the edges of our relationship. I was not always aware of this when it happened. But it did. I don't just mean that on some days we were more irritable with each other, though this is surely part of it. All relationships must have their ups and downs – if nothing else, the 'downs' give the 'ups' meaning – and this can be frustrating, or as we both know, painful. On some days I didn't much feel like talking to you, and I am sure you felt the same.

Losing someone is also a kind of frustration, in that your appetite, which is not yet sated, is deprived of the nourishment it can anticipate, if not quite taste. An affair rudely interrupted, in whatever way, seems unfair and unjust, something that solicits indignation and can work up enough heat to make you want to sue for damages. But the thing I found hard to understand at the time was simply that the contract was not mine or yours to break; we were a means in service to an end, and the means always gets tired, develops arthritis, cardiovascular problems, cancer.

I could not make sense of it. I was upset. It seemed profoundly wrong and painful. But in writing these letters to you, in looking back or reflecting, it feels to me like I can refer our apparently spontaneous and unpremeditated romance to a source of some kind. Sometimes this act of looking back feels like a necessary forward movement towards a final act.

You might reply to all this, and reply with the admonition that this is just a florid form of the words 'I miss you'. These last three words are certainly true, but all the words in this letter (and in the other letters I have written) want to know why.

My dear Coumba, I miss you.

Rémy

In other letters, the purpose was less obviously on display, and I found myself wondering about what he was trying to say.

My Dear Coumba,

Today I spoke to my elderly neighbours, Lisette and Lirienne. Lisette knocked on my door. She asked if I might lend them some rosemary.

"I'm afraid I don't have any rosemary," I replied.

"No rosemary," she said, a little forlorn.

I asked Lisette what she was cooking.

"Something Sicilian," she replied. "Then we will eat it."

"Yes," I said.

"And Lirienne will eat it too. Yes, she will eat it."

"Are you having a feast?" I asked.

Lisette ignored me. Instead she shouted across the hallway.

"Lirienne! Lirienne!" she shouted.

Out came Lirienne.

"Do you have any rosemary," she asked me straight away.

"Ignore her!" said Lisette stubbornly. "Her brain is wasting away!"

"I'm afraid I don't have any rosemary at the moment," I replied.

"And her eyes look like genital warts!" said Lisette.

"It sounds like you are having a feast," I said.

"I should not be at all surprised if Sicilians fart loudly. Like trombones," said Lisette.

"And suffer with terrible indigestion," said Lirienne.

"Oh yes," Lisette agreed.

"Could you manage with something else?" I suggested.

"Oregano, for example?"

Lisette took my hand and patted it. Then she explained.

"No, that would not do. And you must understand that we shall not be admitting any Germans either," she said.

"Those motherfuckers!" shouted Lirienne.

"So we must find some rosemary. But please don't trouble yourself. I am quite sure someone else will help us. And we know already that you are a kind man."

"Thank you," I said.

"Sorry to have troubled you," said Lisette. "Come along Lirienne."

They both turned and, arm in arm, walked across the hallway into their apartment. Before she closed the door, Lirienne looked at me.

"As I close this door, I would ask you not to covet my form."

So, as Lirienne closed the door, I averted my eyes and did not covet her form.

Love

Rémy.

GRAMMAR

"Suppose you were trying to seduce me," said Alice. "How might that work? What would be the etiquette that you seem to be so keen on?"

"I'm not trying to seduce you."

"Which is why I suggested this as an act of imagination."

"Okay ... yes, I see."

We were milling around a boutique. Alice would occasionally clutch at an expensive-looking jacket, hold it to my torso, pull a face and cast it aside before I had time to feel alarmed by the price tag.

I thought about the question for a time. Nothing came to mind. I thought about it some more.

"Well?"

"I don't know," I said eventually. "Honestly, I don't know."

"Well, that's not very impressive," she muttered, half her attention on a mottled-grey blazer.

"What about this one?" she asked, looking a little more hopeful.

"Yes, it looks very good. Nice material," I said, though my heart was clearly not in it.

"You could at least try to have an opinion," she said, tossing it aside.

"Sorry."

"You see, I think we are basically dealing with the same problem here. You can't select any clothes because you don't have enough of a sensibility. You can't seduce me – or imagine how to seduce me – for the same reason."

"I suppose I have always thought that fashion is quite superficial."

"Yes, isn't it wonderful?" she asked, her incisive little eyes stabbing me in the face for the first time in a few hours.

"I mean, in a way, doesn't it abide by exactly what you were saying earlier?"

"How do you mean?"

"It's a game isn't it? You might think that clothes are just a practicality, and that fashion is just an indulgence for those that can afford it. But that's a lot of rubbish. Everyone has a sense of fashion, and everyone is capable of dressing in a particular way, whatever their means. Someone with the right eye – but most importantly the right attitude – will turn a shoestring budget into more than just shoestrings. Your clothes say something about you; they are ... sort of like a code. Even if you aren't trying, and, like you, they succumb to the easiest and most convenient options – that is a statement. And if you accept what I have just said – that everyone can afford to be stylish – then it is quite a sad statement. Do you see what I mean? Because you have reached it by default. Passively and without really trying. You have not chosen your clothes. They have chosen you."

I suddenly felt a sense of purpose about our shopping expedition in a way that I had never felt before about shopping. The room seemed to light up with new-found meaning.

"But if you make the right choices," she continued, "if you select the clothes that are right for you, then magically and all of a sudden, you can become something in the eyes of those around you.

'Of course, I am not saying that you are only defined by your clothes. That would be hopelessly superficial, and it is probably the people that think about clothes in those terms that make you think that all fashion is superficial. But clothes carefully selected are like a street sign, or a set of directions, that point the way to your true character."

Now I was humming with a mixture of excitement and nervous energy.

"Don't you think?"

"I think I see what you mean."

But Alice hadn't finished.

"In a way, what you are really saying when you shop unthinkingly at the supermarket is 'I would rather walk around naked.' It's the mindset of ... it's puritanical. Like you are disdaining outward appearances. But if you go about it in the right way, it's the opposite."

As early as the night before I had started to wonder about the time I had spent with Alice. I didn't doubt for a minute that, without our unusual act of reminiscence, I would never have spoken to her; and I was just as sure that I would not have spoken to anyone else. I might have rambled around, inflicting a few scarcely audible words on passing strangers, but nothing more. The puzzle we shared was the efficient cause of our meeting, but it had, of its own accord and quite naturally, become something else. I couldn't help but think that we were like two people trapped in an elevator who, while very different, just happened to get along quite well. And, I knew, for this reason, that I was grateful for the poor memory that was stringing us along. It was rare, almost unheard of, for me to sustain a conversation with anyone in this way.

As we had entered this shop, I noticed that the shop assistant took the measure of us through pinched eyes that dismissed us coldly, and I found myself imagining her withdrawing to a stock room where she would torture stray animals and small children with the cruel use of a sewing machine. And then I surveyed the sartorial salon, in all its urbane elegance and wealth, in a slightly different way. Were these clothes assembled from the rags scraped off the back of starving children, who had been tortured to death by a sadistic aesthete? Were those buttons a chemical concoction of rats' intestines? Was that man-bag the treated skin of an alley cat?

My mind could have easily kept going, that's how interested I was in clothes or shopping, much less clothes and shopping. For most of the time, I was used to operating at two levels: the public world to which I paid lip service, and in the eyes of which I was mostly ignored, and my own private world of images and impressions borrowed from the stuff and business of the world around me, and which were diced and re-assembled in an unseemly fashion by the unstructured activity of my pointless imagination.

But with Alice, our conversation brought me back to the world of common-sense objects. For what seemed like the first time, a conversation was not a chore, a surreptitious contest of egos, a business matter with its eyes fixed blindly on the score, but something like the phrases in a piece of music that, in combination, produce a pleasing harmony. It was not the greatest compliment I might afford the company of a woman, but Alice had tempered my temptation to see the subversive streak of red scrawled across the front of a t-shirt as the outcome of street pigeons brutally needled.

Alice was shimmering around the shop now, stroking individual items of clothing lightly but affectionately, like they were an extended family of children.

"Or think about it in terms of desire – even love. That's a powerful incentive. You might think that robes are just a more socially acceptable way to arouse desire without actually disrobing; and what we all really aspire to – in terms of sexual desire, I mean – is nudity. Clothes exist to beat a path to the body in its natural state. But it's not true. Without clothes there would be less desire. They don't prevent desire; they enhance it. They intimate, they excite and entice; they stimulate the imagination. And most importantly, they create an obstacle – they create a set of rules to be negotiated and overcome. Compare Marilyn Monroe dressed suggestively with a bunch of hippies dancing naked at an open-air festival: which is the more erotic? Clothes give meaning to desire."

Alice was increasingly lost in her own argument, but I now felt a sense of purpose and mission about shopping, and was keen to start trying things on, or at least forming opinions. I had never before felt such a strong urge to hold an opinion about step-notch lapels.

"In a way it is a shame that there is a perception that you must be either a darling fashionista incapable of seeing beyond matching accessories or you must dress like someone going to church. But they are the same – they come from the same way of thinking."

She looked at me.

"So what do you think now?"

I wanted a vocabulary, and the ability to use it forcefully and persuasively. I wanted to understand the details, the mechanics and technicalities that make the art. And then Alice said something I didn't expect in more ways than one.

"How about something light?" she said.

THE DOG

I spent 230 euros on the jacket, another 70 euros on a shirt, and another 200 euros on a pair of brogue boots. I winced inwardly with each payment, but my new enthusiasm carried me through.

We still had several hours before we were due at the Gare de Lyons, and Alice held the view that I should change before our next performance so that I might 'look the part'. I pointed out that I was playing the part of a man hostile to human society and that, whatever else motivated him, I was sure it was not walking around in an expensive pair of brogue boots (which would almost certainly produce blisters).

"That's not the point," Alice tarted back at me, though she didn't explain what was.

Alice's words were, in any case, delivered like a military manoeuvre so, long trudge as it was, we wandered back to my hotel.

En route, the sky turned heavy, and Alice was convinced

we would get caught in the rain, so she dragged me into a café. Sure enough it started to rain. A chill breeze swept around our ankles.

For the first time since we had met, neither of us said very much. I guessed Alice was tired. I know I was, and even the coffee did little to perk me up. The combination of two nights drinking, and the stress of shopping had started to grind me down. But the tiredness was not unpleasant. It came naturally.

"Sashimi," said Alice.

"I'm sorry?" I said.

"We were talking about sushi yesterday, I think. I seem to remember we were. For me, it's sashimi that really gets me excited."

"Uh huh," I said.

My upper lip scraped the surface of my coffee. Something caught my eye through the window. The same dog we had seen the day before on our way to the restaurant was on the pavement opposite. I was sure it was the same dog. I tried not to look like I was staring (though Alice had her eyes on the table and her mind on secondment to some other purpose).

I pretended to be watching the world go by, but my eyes returned again and again to the dog. Each time I looked in its direction, the more certain I became that it was the same dog. It had the same colouring, and exactly the same marks. It had the same tentative but hopeful wag of the tail, a faint suggestion of misplaced faith in the kindness of human beings.

It was lingering around the same spot, with no obvious reason and for no obvious purpose. It would take a few steps in our direction, sidestep some well-toned but apathetic French legs, pause to contemplate the world and maybe check out an interesting smell in the gutter, and then take a few steps in the other direction. This incidental study of the same territory was tireless. It looked like the dog was hostage to a purpose it didn't fully understand, a little like the sight of a street-walker who only suggests the trappings of a more unseemly world.

The busy manner of its movement gave the impression that the dog was muttering to itself under its breath.

Occasionally the dog would make a futile upwards enquiry into the indifference of the street's pedestrians.

"Spare any food? A sausage perhaps? Scrap of bread? Something like that? I'm not particular about vegetables, you know. What are you wearing? Is that a rodent on your head? I mean human beings really are the most obscene and ridiculous ... good grief that woman smells like she has smeared herself in orange-flavoured chocolate. Oh and by the way you missed a patch with the razor, dear. Talk about a dog's life!"

I looked silently through the window as Alice hung her head over the table, her body obviously engulfed by tiredness. This irritating distance from the dog made me want to stride out of the café, across the street, sit down on the pavement and address it face to face, just as we had done the day before.

"Hello again."

"Oh hello," the dog would reply.

"Look, I just wanted to apologise. We were trying to follow you yesterday, but we seemed to lose sight of you through a crowd of Germans."

"Well, Germans aren't known for their liberal territorialism," the dog would reply. "But it's all right. I wasn't expecting you to keep following me."

"But we could tell that you were trying to get our attention. And then all of a sudden ... what was it you wanted to ... were you trying to tell us something?"

"Well, you know, I would love to stop and chat, but a hound has to hunt, if you see what I mean. It's lovely to see you again, of course. But I haven't had a bean to eat in the last twenty four hours, and that causes the most mighty rumblings from l'interieur."

"Of course, of course, how inconsiderate of me. Well, I tell you what, why don't you let me buy you something."

"I couldn't allow that."

"I insist."

"No really that isn't ... what did you have in mind?"

"Could I buy you sushi, perhaps?"

Witnessing myself have this conversation with the dog from across the street in the café, as Alice slouched further towards the inevitable outcome of her fatigue, I admonished myself for making such a foolish suggestion in my daydream. Why, of all things, the dog would want sushi, I didn't know. I expected my lazy mind was just recalling my last words with Alice. Even so, my imagination replied in an unexpected way.

"That's kind of you," the dog would reply. "I believe sushi is properly complemented by horseradish and I find that quite indigestible."

"You surprise me."

"Oh yes. I suppose people think that dogs' stomachs can cope with any old muck, but not mine. Years of destitution mean that one cannot afford to be too particular, but eating an irregular diet can also take its toll."

"And horseradish doesn't agree with you?"

"Like you wouldn't believe."

"Well I never."

"Incidentally, I can't help but notice something."

"What's that?"

"You seem to be having an imaginary conversation with a stray dog."

"You noticed that did you."

"Yes, I am quite perspicacious about these sort of things."

I congratulated the dog on his commendable empiricism.

"That doesn't set any alarm bells ringing for you, then?" asked the dog.

"To tell you the truth, the reason I came over here just now was very simple. I was wondering something, while Alice – that's the fast-fading feminine form I was sitting with in the café over the road – was slumping in her seat. Do you know what I was wondering?"

"Do tell."

"Alice and I have been experiencing some strange things in the course of the last day or so. And, to tell you the truth,

I was wondering if you had anything to do with them."

"What makes you say that?"

"A hunch really. Nothing more than that. Just a hunch."

"I am quite an extraordinary dog, it must be said," said the dog modestly.

"Yes, that's what I mean."

"Did you know I can lick my own testicles?"

Before my waning concentration descended into semi-unconscious gibberish, I paid the bill.

As Alice was collecting her things, she made a public offering of a new thought.

"What do you think will happen next?" she asked. "In our little story, I mean?"

I had been trying to remember, I told her, but the harder I tried, the more tired my memory became. So my answers were 'No', and 'I don't know what will happen next.'

"I wonder if we will remember anything."

And then, curiously, she glanced over her shoulder, and across the street at the spot where, until a moment ago, the dog had been sniffing around. But he was no longer there.

Alice was no more communicative between the café and the hotel, stopping only to ask me whether we were going in the right direction.

"So you aren't staying far from the Moulin Rouge, then?" she said, inspecting the streets like a tourist.

The rain had eased off slightly, leaving only a light patter through which we wandered more or less indifferently. My feet were hurting. My arms were aching. I wanted to sit down. Or lie down. Or sleep.

I seemed to lose sight of the dog when we left the café, but I noticed that it had at some point re-appeared. I could see it again on the pavement opposite, weaving around legs, perhaps stopping momentarily in response to a shout, another curious sound or the intrusion of a smell. Despite these small distractions, it still managed somehow to keep pace with us. Naturally, this made me think it was following us – which was, in truth, what I wanted to think. But the dog did not look over its shoulder, or at any point that I noticed, give any indication that it had seen us. I thought that perhaps this was deliberate. Perhaps it thought that we had shunned it the day before, and was now trying a more subtle and diplomatic way to win hearts.

Whatever the explanation, that the dog appeared to be following us, only aroused my suspicion further, and made me think that there was much more to this than met the eye. It was all too uncanny. Surely it could not just be a coincidence?

Alice walked a little ahead of me. I would glance at her (or around her) to see if she had seen, or acknowledged, the dog at any point. But she was not paying enough attention.

"I must be getting old. I'm so tired."

"I don't think your age has anything to do with it."

We walked a little further, and turned a corner.

"This is it," I said, gesturing further up the street.

As I followed Alice into the hotel lobby, I glanced across the road once again. The dog was still trotting about, but apparently indifferent to us or anyone.

My hotel room was on the top floor of the hotel, with a

skylight that overlooked the rooftops.

I opened the skylight, threw my bags on the floor, and turned to find that Alice had already disintegrated on my bed. She lay back, cruciform but at peace. I just caught her eyes closing.

I shuffled about the room for a while, wishing I also had a bed on which to collapse. My eyes found an armchair. But before I went looking for comfort, I returned to the skylight, stuck my head out of the window, trying to spy the street below. It was a little difficult to make out, but I thought I could just catch sight of the dog, ferreting about in the dirt and desperation beneath the clouds.

Back in my armchair, I looked across the room at Alice asleep. Was it unusual to invite women twice your age (or thereabouts) back to your hotel room? And who was she? These were all questions I was asking myself, or, more accurately, questions I thought I should be asking myself. But my sense of propriety, already diminished after years of feeling generally inadequate, did not find much traction. Maybe I was just too tired, because not long after I sank into the armchair and the sleep that had been waiting there for me all afternoon.

Sleep is always misleading and disorienting, but even more so during the day. I woke to find Alice leaning back against a chest of drawers, staring at me. I didn't know where I was, who I was staring at, or even if – or what – I had just been dreaming.

"You sleep like a drunk," said Alice.

I was just beginning to realise that Alice was Alice, that

Alice was in Paris, which meant that I was too. I was also trying to work out how long I had been asleep.

"Oh ... sorry," I mumbled.

"That's all right. It's just I would say you look more slovenly than comfortable."

I wiped my mouth, expecting to find drool.

"You sleep like Jesus on the cross," I said, without thinking too much about it.

She smiled.

"What time is it?" I asked.

"Time to get dressed," she said, raising her eyebrows.

"I am dressed."

"In that case, it's time to get re-dressed."

"Okay. Are we going straight to the station? Do I really need to look so expensive?"

"Well first of all, don't flatter yourself that you do look expensive, and second, don't underestimate its importance. It's important to make the effort. You can't imagine what it's like to seduce me unless you look good."

"You've latched onto that idea, haven't you?"

"It's something to flirt with."

I leaned forward in my chair, a little uneasy.

"Would you like me to leave the room?" she asked.

I stood up and pulled up the bags of clothes I had thrown to the floor.

"No, you don't need to do that. I'll get changed in the salle de bain."

I got re-dressed.

"I don't really want you to seduce me. You know that,

don't you?" she said through the door.

"Yes, I know," I said.

"I'm too old," she explained.

I returned to the room, sat in the armchair, and began putting on the boots.

"I'm sorry, I don't mean to go on about it, but there is something about being alone in a young man's bedroom. It plays tricks on the mind."

I pulled forcefully on my boot laces. There was a pause.

"Am I making you uncomfortable?" she asked, sounding indeterminately hopeful.

I stood up, pulled on the light – but very expensive – blazer.

"What do you think?"

She moved towards me in zigzags, assessing me from all angles. She took a few steps back.

"Turn around," she instructed.

I turned around.

"Yes," she muttered contemplatively. "And turn again. To face me."

I returned to my original position.

She took a few steps forward, offering me the outstretched arms of a congratulatory hug. She placed her hands on my shoulders and ran them down my arms. What this gesture was meant to achieve I was not sure.

She took two steps back again, examined me, and pulled a face.

"No good?" I asked.

"No, no ... it's not that. It suits you well. But ... well, men don't always know how to wear their clothes."

She recovered her retreat, and put her face in mine, reaching around me with both arms. First, she placed her hands on my sides, then she leaned closer so that her chest dug into mine, gripped the lower part of my new jacket, and gave it a few sharp tugs. Her eyes interrogated mine, suggesting that this was an unnecessarily theatrical excuse to get her paws on me, and see how I might react. I didn't really react.

"You're so ... tense," she said.

She turned around, and walked all the way across the room to the bed. She sat on its edge to carry out a full inspection. She sized me up. She told me to turn once more.

"Yes, it does suit you well."

It sounded like a perfunctory compliment, but I could feel a slim insinuation of pride in response to her words. I didn't feel shallow about it either.

We prepared to leave.

"It's strange, don't you think?"

"What's that?"

"Suppose I were your age. Or ... well, of a more approachable age. I mean, I wouldn't have come back to your hotel room. I wouldn't have fallen asleep on your bed, watched you and helped you get dressed. I couldn't have touched you in the way I did just now. Not with the same business-like confidence anyway."

"Was that business-like?"

"I would have been nervous and possibly a little excited. I might have wanted to touch you. I might even have wanted you to touch me. Perhaps you might have wanted to touch me. Perhaps we might have ended up fucking on your bed ..."

She seemed to want a reply to that.

"... Perhaps," I said, a little late.

"My confidence, my age, and the boldness that comes with that destroys the potential for love. Don't you think?"

"Well, I suppose other things have brought us together."

"Yes, I suppose that's right. There's nothing quite like the naivety and innocence of relative equals," she reflected nostalgically.

Alice didn't look sad exactly, but something softened or dented her hard edges.

THE ORPHAN

My Dear Coumba,

There was once a young boy. He was no more than eight or nine. His father had died many years ago, shortly after he was born.

One day the boy got back from school to find two men waiting for him. They had come with bad news. His mother – his only surviving guardian – had been killed in a fire that had claimed the lives of many others. So, from that day on, he was an orphan.

Though an orphan, the local community took the boy into its care. Three families took it in turns to invite him into their homes each evening. They would sit him down at the dinner table, and feed him in whatever way they could. Sometimes, if the evening ran late, he would sleep the night in an armchair; but at the end of most evenings, he would walk home to the empty house of his parents.

At the end of one such evening, he came home to find a

basket of freshly baked bread on his doorstep. It was covered with a towel to preserve the heat. The boy did not know what to make of it. He waited some moments to see if anyone might claim the bread. Eventually, he thought "Well, the bread will only go cold if I leave it on the doorstep, and if it belongs to someone, they can always knock."

So the boy took the bread inside and stowed it away safely in the old stone parlour. The basket he left by the front door with the collection of his mother's now unworn shoes.

In the coming days, no-one came to claim the bread, and since it would have otherwise gone to waste, the boy ate it for breakfast with ham and gherkins.

Some days later when he returned from another evening meal, he noticed something unusual as he entered the house. The basket in which he had found the bread had gone. And a pair of his mother's shoes was clearly missing. He searched around the house to make sure he had not moved the missing items without thinking about it. He could not find them anywhere. This made him worry. He began to think that he had been burgled, but could not find anything else missing.

Something told the boy to keep the business of the bread basket and the disappearing shoes to himself, so he did not mention it to his neighbours when he next went around for dinner. And he was glad he had not mentioned it, because when he returned to his house, he found that the bread basket was, once again, resting on his doorstep, and tucked snugly inside it was another freshly baked loaf. The boy blinked in disbelief, and looked over his shoulder to see if anyone was watching him secretly. He could see no-one.

Inside the house, almost as he had expected, his mother's shoes had returned to their former place, next to the door.

That evening established the pattern: the boy would return home at the end of an evening to find bread in the basket; as soon as he had finished the bread, he would leave the basket by the door; the basket, along with his mother's shoes, would disappear for a while, only to reappear later with more freshly made bread.

For many months he kept this pattern secret. In fact, he held it close, unwilling to let it escape into the community, fearing what they might make of it. His knowledge somehow made him feel warm, rather than threatened. It did not seem sinister. If anything, it filled some of the empty space that the death of his mother had left behind.

News of the mysterious parcels of bread only ever reached the rest of the community when a neighbour happened to notice the boy collecting the basket. The next day, the neighbour asked the boy how he had come by the bread. The boy wanted to lie. He wanted anything but to reveal his secret. But he could not lie. The longer the boy kept his silence, the more his neighbour looked stern.

An almost audible whisper spread throughout the community. They spoke in hushed tones across the breakfast table or on their way back from work. The excitement and curiosity was almost palpable, and all eyes were fixed on the front door to the boy's home. Everyone wanted to catch sight of the mysterious person (or persons) delivering the parcels of bread.

So the entire community watched, as they continued to

talk about it behind closed doors. The parcels kept arriving, but no-one ever caught sight of a person depositing them.

This, thought the community, was a curious and marvellous thing; and while they all shared the same reaction, they looked upon it and came to think of it, in different ways. Some – the more superstitious – believed that the spirit of the boy's dead mother was delivering the bread. More considered and sceptical individuals thought that, while the events were meant to look like the work of a revenant, it was more likely that someone had taken it upon themselves to give the boy this impression, so that it might comfort him at this traumatic and unsettling time. Still others, suggested that this was the work of someone else, a charity or a religious institution determined to safeguard the welfare of the young man discreetly. Some thought he had an unknown guardian who, for some undisclosed reason, wished to remain unknown. And some said that the boy was baking bread for himself, and that the strange events were only a desperate cry for attention.

These interpretations kept coming. They would sometimes seem to multiply over a single conversation. It nearly got to a point where the number of opinions equalled the number of people in the community. Each carried their views about the boy and the parcels of baked bread. Everyone had absorbed the story and moulded it around their rituals and routines.

The boy, meanwhile, was in much the same situation. His neighbours' gossip and speculation had done nothing to explain the events since his mother's death. He had once heard the expression that 'a problem shared is a problem halved'. But, in his case, he thought this wasn't true. The death of his mother had left him alone, but this nest of rumour and interpretation only made him feel more alone.

One day he felt sure that someone would say he had engineered his mother's death, just so that the community might spend their lives talking about him, or else they would claim that his mother had faked her own death for the same reason. He even began to witness how quickly opinions in the community could turn from sympathy to suspicion, to something like condemnation. It was strange, he thought, how these events and their meaning could acquire a life of their own. But, with each experience, and as the meaning of events became more complex and overlaid, the harder he found it to make sense of the situation at all. He even heard it said that someone had denied the events had ever taken place.

The more the boy thought about how he might challenge or defend one of the many interpretations, the more dispiriting and futile it seemed. The gossip and speculation could not be tamed. Even if he were to sit down and discuss things rationally, and even if he were to reach some sort of agreement, he felt sure that the chattering would soon resurface.

None of this stopped the boy thinking for himself. He would spend evenings studying the basket and the shoes, casting his eyes over the house in search of displacements, fingerprints or signs of surreptitious movements photographed in the motes of dust. He would pace up and down in his front room, arms crossed behind his back, and head hanging thoughtfully, as he worked the facts into a meticulous musical rhythm.

One evening when he returned to find a fresh basket of bread and his mother's shoes returned to his usual place, he spent an hour walking up and down in front of the shoes, studying them from different angles, observing all the wrinkles, stretches and signs of infirmity. Eventually he knelt down, and sniffed inside them. He caught the familiar smell of his mother.

All in all, these events left the boy with one overriding sentiment: he felt that he was a secret his neighbours had created.

Of all theories about the bread, he preferred the crudest. He liked to think that it was his mother delivering the parcels; and that she was still, in some way, watching over him. He also liked to think, in his more mischievous moments, that his mother had planned the events, not just to ensure he was properly fed, but knowing the reaction it would provoke. He liked to imagine his mother carrying out this little routine and laughing at it all.

All my love
Rémy

ON A STATION

"Do you ever regret what you did?"

"How do you mean?"

"I mean have you ever regretted coming here?"

This question clearly planted the seed of an idea in Alice's mind. She squinted at me.

We were killing time in the shadow of the Gare de Lyons' famous clock tower, hoping that, before we met once again with Rémy, the place would help the fuller memory to give way. Our efforts were more fruitful than the time we had spent mainly preoccupied with the easily preoccupying sex-in-running-shorts from earlier in the day. The building of the station, like the building of the church, was part of the memory. It was firmly ingrained. Unlike the church, the station was a famous landmark but there was more to it than this; it went together with Alice and words that I knew were waiting to trip from the tip of my tongue, albeit not at my instruction.

"Not at all," replied Alice. "I don't have any regrets. It was the right thing to do as far as I'm concerned. No, more than that. It was the moral thing to do. Before I left I was just living a kind of slow death. That's an offence to your existence. And it's a pernicious society that allows it to happen at all."

Alice's squint – it looked like someone was pulling on her eyes with a cocktail stick from the inside – suggested to me that this remark of mine and her, very strident, response had planted the seed of a thought, but that I would have to wait before it burgeoned and responded to the temptations of nature.

Then, to my surprise, self-doubt took her off course.

"Though I sometimes wonder," she said.

She stopped, perhaps trying to compose her thoughts, or considering whether to compose her thoughts.

"I know for certain that I have felt like that for much of my adult life. But I recently ... I don't know, I suppose it's just getting old – recently I don't feel I have the energy to sustain that commitment to my rebellion. To live in a permanent state of revolt requires ... you need energy and will that I am not sure I have any more. And I don't suppose I am really committed to that. But now that I look back on it – you know, the way I used to feel and to some extent the way I still feel – the more it seems groundless somehow."

"Groundless?" I asked.

"I mean if you react strongly to something that can be powerful. It can stir you to all kinds of things. But it's a passive pose to strike. Your actions are defined in reaction to something else. And I think ... sometimes I wonder how different things might have been if my behaviour took its orders from my own initiative. I sometimes wonder how that might look and feel; and if it might have been better."

I didn't really want to hear this qualification. Somehow a rebellion that lacks confidence just isn't a rebellion.

"Anyway, I'm not sure I really want to talk about this," she said.

This suggested that Alice, too, didn't particularly want to hear herself say these things. The mere suggestion that she was not everything she at first seemed exposed a crack out of which might crawl an ugly and long-tentacled identity crisis.

Just as a full frontal encounter with a freight train is fairly unambiguous, an encounter with Alice was, generally speaking, much the same. On collision, I seemed to lie under her for an interminable amount of time, pinned to the ground by an endless succession of forward movement. As the champion, apologist or warrior for a political cause, I thought she would be formidable, and I wondered if, in fact, she had not missed a career as a strategic missile deployed by the big-boss men of national politics to solve short-term problems through muscle and intimidation. Alice, in all circumstances, would possess, control, and assert in ways that were almost incidental to the object of each verb.

It was this that made some of the things she had said to me over the last day so strange. She had, in different ways, intimated regret, frustration, lack of confidence, unhappiness, even suicide. Was there a paradox here? Could such apparent confidence sit so easily with despair? At times in the course of our conversation, I had even thought that Alice was laying everything out to anyone who might listen, in order to satisfy an internal neurosis of some kind.

But this last conversation also made me stop and think about myself. When Alice told me her story of rebellion and breakaway, I had been attracted to it, and intrigued by her. This ability to respond to stifling authoritarianism with two fingers appealed to me precisely because it was something I would never do, even if, from time to time, I might fantasise about it. In some ways, she embodied a rock-and-roll mentality that I was still young enough to respect. So hearing her call it into question made me feel uncomfortably grown up.

To hear her talk as though, despite her conviction, something was not quite right about her life of protest and polemic, hinted that the freedom she coveted, and which I envied, was always one step ahead of any attempt to possess it. And unnervingly, disappointingly, the extent of these thoughts led full circle: my stoical and uninspired life on the average wage, inhabiting the average working week, and spending the average amount at the supermarket for a single young professional, showed some clearer understanding of the elusive liberation I could sense only faintly. If Alice, in perfect contradiction, wanted to arrest it altogether, I understood the contradiction and had given up the chase.

Silence filled the air. I tried hard not to scratch my forehead awkwardly.

Then the dog appeared.

We both noticed him at the same time, but I had not seen

from where he had come. He stood, side-on next to us, his head kinked around, looking from me to Alice and back again. When I glanced across at her, in a mixture of surprise and excitement, it looked like Alice was about to say something like 'Well, what are you doing here?', but before she could speak, the dog lowered his head and walked away. This simple movement was done solemnly. I wanted to call – or even run – after him, but before I could overcome the long delay between my brain and body, Rémy turned up.

"So are you ready for episode two?" he said, a layer of relish in his voice.

"Oh hello," said Alice.

"I'm not sure if I ever got it right: are you lovers or a mother and son? You can never be sure. I'm sure you can never be sure!"

"We are neither," said Alice flatly. "We don't know each other."

"You don't know each other?"

Rémy gave a little laugh that poked at the corners of his mouth.

"You just ... you are two people who just happened to bump into each other?"

"Almost."

"I don't understand."

This admission gave Alice something to play with, and she seized on the situation with the predatory instinct of a feline hunter listening to the chirruping lyric of birdsong.

"Oh you don't understand, do you?" she asked.

"No, Madame," replied Rémy, suddenly baffled.

"It seems a little confusing to you, does it?"

"Perhaps."

"And you are interested to know how this young man and I came into each other's company? Since you are due to profit by that company, I suspect it is only natural that you would be."

"Your affairs are your own. I only ... "

" ... no, no, it's only natural, like I say."

"As you like – let us say that I am curious; but that comes only from my professional interest in you."

Alice tied her eyes around Rémy.

"And yet, I must say that yesterday, I was a little alarmed ..." he confessed. "You say that you don't know each other, but I feel sure that we – I mean all three of us – must have met before somewhere."

"You don't know the half of it," said Alice, and then she gave him more scrutiny. "Or perhaps you do."

Rémy thought about this for a moment, and then said:

"You're speaking in riddles, Madame."

Rémy was, as far as I could tell, wearing exactly the same clothes as the day before. His hair, scraggy and uncombed, curled over his scalp, like pine cones glued to a rubber head in an infant's art project. The appearance of grime lay about his skin. But, once again, this lack of self-respect could not disguise his innate poise and dignified carriage. It was very odd. I thought he must have had to really cultivate his dishevelled appearance. Where other men would reach for the aftershave and the nasal-hair trimmers, did he run down to the street each morning and roll in the mud? Or perhaps it was even more contrived. Perhaps he had a servant who would collect dirt in a jar and, under instruction, throw it in the face of his master with a flash of repressed venom.

This all made the nosegay of carnations Rémy was carrying look out of place; but I guessed quickly, and correctly, that they were props sharp to the point of our next scene.

"Well then," said Alice, "we are in your hands."

Rémy turned reflective. His mind witnessed more than the matter at hand.

"I sometimes think that death comes when you stop being afraid of it."

Alice looked worried that the disquisitions of continental philosophy might be about to rear their closely shaved head and start using words like 'discourse' and 'diachronic' as a matter of common parlance.

"No less recondite for being slightly off the point and gloomy," she said. "Does it loom large in the drama?"

"No," said Rémy philosophically, "I was just thinking about it."

"Well then," said Alice, ushering him to business.

"We must go into the station first," he explained, his mind still recovering its centre of gravity.

The Gare de Lyons was a harder crowd to work. We were in full view of the station's many travellers, its staff, not to mention CCTV cameras and armed security. These conditions did nothing to ease the pressure.

Rémy gave us our brief. The countess had been away in the country, on the pretext of visiting relatives, when in fact she was only trying to avoid detection and capture.

We were to understand that at this stage in the drama, the couple's romance had only the sureness of infant legs. The countess, wise to the movements of her hunter, had written to the watchmaker, ahead of her return to Paris. She asked him, in her letter, if he would be gallant enough to meet her off the train, underneath the station clock.

So the scene began as I waited underneath the station clock, and tried not to imagine that people were looking at me. We had found it hard to communicate at all when we first arrived on the station; the constant noise and announcements, the unstructured assault of people standing around each other, and the general sense of disorientation in which this enveloped us, meant that we survived only by unfinished sentences and pointing.

To create the impression that Alice had just arrived off a train, she approached me from a distance. I was sure the gendarmes would approach me as I waited, simply because I looked so shifty and conspicuous. Even if they thought I was innocent, I could imagine a highly strung policeman irritated by the distraction from the causes and instigators of real crime; and, I wondered whether, in the eyes of French law, just looking like I was up to no good, in a way that diverted the police from the duties of keeping the public peace, might be a crime.

I imagined the scene: the police strong-arming me towards an oubliette smelling of bodily fluids, as Alice followed hastily, trying to explain in lilted French, that we were only performing a piece of street theatre mysteriously connected to our failure to remember how we knew each other.

"Oh yes, that's what they all say!" I could hear the police snort.

My mind painted details. I imagined something cultured and effete about the policeman who escorted me towards incarceration. I imagined him leading me towards a box-room, the starch taken out of it by floral wallpaper and hand-knitted cardigans resting snugly on the back of interrogation chairs. And, in my mind, my police escort struggled to contain an effeminate manner behind his grizzled facade: perhaps he would kiss me on both cheeks and seek my opinion on nineteenth century light opera before breaking my ribs to teach me a lesson.

Rémy explained that there were more than two figures in this second of the three scenes; but the third was a menacing spectre that cast a shadow from the background. This was the undercover assassin tasked with hunting down the countess. Rémy said that he would undertake to play this role so that our scene might 'run smoothly'.

"How do you know it will run smoothly? We don't know what we are going to say" I asked him.

"Didn't it last time?" was his reply. "And I have to say that listening to the two of you yesterday, I would never have guessed that you didn't know the lines you were speaking. Often my clients want to run through it several times as they develop and refine the details of the scenario. But sometimes, when the circumstances are right, the words just flow. I must admit that I didn't think that, in your case, the circumstances were right. You have surprised me."

Alice approached through the subterfuge of the countess' disguise. In the same way as the day before, things started to fall into place. The memory accompanied the countess' return to Paris. The disquieting part of each step that Alice took towards me was that the memory took me over. I had no say in the matter. Even if I had flexed a muscle of objection, I would have been almost powerless to resist the scene that played out. I was a puppet in service to some other design.

I found Alice looking at me with an odd expression, part-irritated, part-anxious.

And then, a little hesitantly, she kissed me.

COUNTESS
Thank you for meeting me. It was good of you to come.

WATCHMAKER
Not at all. I was glad to. Did you have a pleasant time with your relatives? I expect they were delighted by your surprise visit!

COUNTESS
They were pleased. And surprised.

WATCHMAKER
It's hardly surprising that they were surprised. Even I was surprised by the sudden way you abandoned the city.

COUNTESS
Sometimes a surprise is the most pleasant way to see someone.

WATCHMAKER
Very modern.

COUNTESS
You don't approve?

WATCHMAKER
I wouldn't say that.

COUNTESS
Should we leave?

WATCHMAKER
You seem distressed. Is something the matter?

COUNTESS
Oh, it's nothing, I'm sure. I'm just restless. I need a walk.

WATCHMAKER
You were behaving like this before you left in such a hurry.

COUNTESS
What do you mean?

WATCHMAKER
I ... before we ... I want to say something that has been on my mind.

COUNTESS
Then you should say it.

WATCHMAKER
You might remember that, on the day we met, I had lost my friend. This was especially upsetting for me, because that friend was my only surviving friend. Life, I find, has been cruel. Sometimes I have invited it. As you know, my parents died when I was young, and my only surviving kin live in London (and I rarely hear from them). So I am largely alone in a world that can seem forbidding, threatening and ready to steal from me even the smallest possessions of any value I have acquired.

This, I want to say, is the person you have come to know, however briefly. And I might have thick skin but ... but it is not callused. There is only a simple way to put it ... I have become very fond of you. But there are certain things about your behaviour – these go back to the very first day that we met – that should give me cause for concern, and might even lead me to think that, for a reason I cannot know, you are ...

COUNTESS
What?

WATCHMAKER
… using me. Forgive me if I do you an injustice, and this suspicious mind of mine has led me only to a suspicious habit of mind rather than a well-read account of how things truly stand.

Alice paused.

COUNTESS
I understand why you have said these things. And, in the end, you must judge me as you think best. Your words are very direct. Can't I persuade you?

WATCHMAKER
You can try.

COUNTESS
You are a believer, Lanier. You want to believe. Your eyes are fixed on a single object. With an unshakeable will. But I think you are scared. Which is why you shut yourself away. Otherwise you would have to compromise. I want you to believe in me. But only you can do that. That's a risk you will have to take.

She placed the palm of her hand against my cheek.

WATCHMAKER
I'm sorry to confront you. You have only just alighted from

the train.

COUNTESS
I'm sure you were right to.

WATCHMAKER
I thought it best to tackle the subject directly.

COUNTESS
Yes.

WATCHMAKER
But I'm sure we have stayed here long enough.

I turned on my heel and, in the same motion, extended my elbow to Alice. In the view I vacated she – or the countess – caught a glimpse of her would-be assassin, played in our recreation, by Rémy. He had wandered close to us, but, from the way he was looking around, appeared not to have seen us. Alice summoned her best imitation of panic, and pulled me back forcefully to where I had been standing, so that she could hide behind me.

COUNTESS
Please!

WATCHMAKER
Whatever's the matter?

COUNTESS
Nothing ... I ... I just ... I was not expecting ... I ... I suppose I ... this was a special moment, don't you think? I would like it to last a little longer.

I was surprised because things went slightly wrong at this point; everything else about the scene – just like the scene from the day before – was so seamless and contrived that it seemed inconceivable it could run anything other than smoothly. The slight blip did not put us off; neither did it break the hypnotic flow of dialogue.

Rémy moved to stand behind me, still ignorant of the countess' whereabouts. Alice pulled me to one side so that she might take shelter behind me. At this point, I was clearly meant to intuit deception at the very point my character had just put it to rest. So I recoiled. Alice followed my movements, hiding from Rémy. But as I stepped backwards I more or less trod on a small Japanese woman, who hit me (quite hard) with the flat of her mobile phone.

I apologised, and the small Japanese woman said something that I took to be insulting.

But even with this interruption, I simply turned around and picked up the pieces where we had left off.

WATCHMAKER
Who is that man?

COUNTESS
What man?

WATCHMAKER
That man. You were hiding from him. Who is ...?

COUNTESS
... I don't know what you mean.

WATCHMAKER
You obviously know him. Don't lie to me! You were frightened of him.

COUNTESS
I ... no ... you're ...

WATCHMAKER
Is he your husband?

COUNTESS
Don't be ridiculous! Of course he's not my ...

WATCHMAKER
... then who is he?

COUNTESS
He's no-one. Someone waiting for a train.

WATCHMAKER
You're lying! I knew you were deceiving me. Why? Who are you?

COUNTESS
I don't know ... I don't ... I wasn't ... yes ... I should ... I can't lie ... yes, you are right. Of course you are right. I must tell you ...

WATCHMAKER
... you admit it ...

COUNTESS
... I must tell you the truth.

WATCHMAKER
Yes ...

I paused.

WATCHMAKER
... but then again, no. What difference does it make?

And with these remarks, the scene came to an end, on the understanding that the watchmaker had abandoned the countess on the station.

The shell-shocked look with which Alice looked at me was familiar; but, as Rémy approached, his expression made it clear that he was now sharing our experience:

he had become part of the same memory, and spoiled with interest.

“We need to talk,” he said simply.

A FRACAS

Alice was carefully selecting mushrooms, and then placing them one-by-one in her mouth, stopping every now and then to sip from a glass of white wine which she had encouraged me to choose.

In a way that it had not before, an invisible object of shared interest had formed between us. We were both aware of it. The day before we had followed the disorder of the day's events, partly in the belief that either some mistake was blurring the edges of our understanding or a logical and verifiable explanation was close at hand. Since neither of us had really believed what was going on, we had been happy to go with it. But now the strange circumstances of the weekend had crystallised. They had become more real and adamantine. Something was at play.

I forked a noisette of lamb purposefully.

Between our bursts of conversation I thought I could detect distrustful but searching looks. Alice would squint or rein her eyeballs back across the table, not quite capable of suppressing her doubt that I was not everything I had at first seemed. And, once or twice, I just noticed my mind probing at the surface of Alice to see what might lie underneath. The mood walked a fine line between suspicion and quietly amused curiosity. This was the peculiarity; it was only from the narrow perspective of a sane and judicious conceit of mind that everything looked suspicious. We were haunted by the echo of a madman's laughter; and the laughter was surprisingly infectious.

"Do you have any regrets?" Alice asked me.

Her look suggested that the question was designed to lay bare my ulterior motives.

"What about?" I replied.

"Do you regret that you came here? For the weekend?"

"No," I said straight away, knowing that I was speaking the truth.

"And why do you suppose you came here?"

The same second layer of purpose lay behind her question.

"I ..." I began, but didn't finish.

"... I wonder about things," she cut me off. "I wonder. I wonder what all of this can mean. Don't you wonder what it can mean?"

"I suppose I do."

"Look you have to at least play along with this. You have to. Don't you see? I'm just about prepared to accept that neither of us really know what's going on – though I'm not ruling out that you might know more than you are letting on. But if we're both in the dark, then I think we have to run with it; something unusual is happening between us and that must mean that we should lay our cards on the table. I'm not sure you have really done that. You've got to respond. So I'm going to ask the question again: why did you come here?"

"Can't I just be on holiday?"

"No! I mean, come on, if that's the truth then I'm going to spit on you and slap you in the face just for being so dull!"

I tried to look unflappable.

"Would you like to order some red wine?"

She stood up, reached across the table and slapped me hard across the cheek. No-one had ever done this to me before, and I was so shocked that I scarcely caught what she said when she sat down. I could see pretty much the entire restaurant turn to look at me, and only gradually reclaim their privacy.

"Yes, they are looking at you! What did you expect? But who gives a fuck?! You do! But I don't ... I don't. If it really matters, when it comes to it – if it's to make the right point – then I don't give a fuck! Why do you care? What do you think will happen? Are they going to whisper things to each other and make pointed comments in the car on their way home? These people you have never met before and will most likely never see again? And don't pretend that you don't know what I am talking about. You do. Of course you do. Just like you came here for a reason. I know it. I can smell it. It's like some rotten inner core that extrudes through your pores. And I'm going to get to the bottom of it."

I had managed to calm down a little as she spoke.

"Or perhaps you'd prefer rosé?" I asked.

I was facing the vanguard of a martial action. I wanted to parry it away.

"This is what this is all about ..." she said, pointing out the distance between us. "... I'm sure of it. It's no accident. There's some ... some connection. I know it. I can feel it. So don't stare back at me with that masquerade of blankness. You are as curious about this as I am; I can tell!"

I floundered.

"I don't know ...I have been to Paris before, but it was a while ago."

"And?" she prompted.

Her voice channelled the sound of her foot tapping.

"Honestly, I think you might be ... I'm not sure there's a ..."

"What are you saying? Just say it."

"I'm not sure there's a connection. Between my visit and ... you know ..."

"No, I think there is."

"You don't think you might be looking for a connection?"

"Of course I'm looking for a connection. That's exactly what I'm doing. That doesn't mean there isn't one. Why us? What is it that we have in common? And I can see something ... you're not telling me something. I can see it. I want to know what it is."

I let Alice's anxious search for the truth swill around me for a while as I thought about what she was asking.

"I don't think I have really given it that much thought," I said, even though this was a lie. "But since I last came here, Paris has only been a place I have read about or seen in films. And I think that was why I wanted to come. I mean there's something about it as a city of romance that made me want to visit. Not that I expect to find someone who will hold my hand here. That's not what I mean. It's like the gestures, the rituals and the etiquette of romance are written into the buildings. Most other guys my age are married, in some cases with children. Well, I'm not .... But coming to Paris is like some sort of acknowledgement of a heart that can't find a home."

"Uh huh."

"I'm not very good at explaining it."

Alice gulped.

"So that's why you came?"

I could see her mind working this over. She tried to relate it to the problem she had placed at the centre of our conversation.

She chuckled to herself.

"What?" I said.

"Nothing. Sorry, I shouldn't laugh."

"What d'you mean?" I said, laughing too.

"Are you aware how ... ? You're so uptight. Is it deliberate? It can't be deliberate."

"It isn't deliberate."

"It's strange to find someone so pre-Lady Chatterley in this day and age."

I took a sip of water.

"No," she continued, "I'm sure it isn't deliberate. But I can't help it. Your whole bearing bothers me. Can I be candid?"

"Why do you suddenly feel the need to ask?"

"It's so obvious. I mean come on. Just find some flighty minx who will fuck your brains out for a bit and get all that nervous energy out of your system."

I took another sip of water.

"Not a remedy that appeals?" she asked.

"I think earlier, you said that by wearing this jacket I was a little like Marilyn Monroe dressed suggestively. That by dressing up in an appropriate way the art of concealment might make the object concealed more enticing."

"So?"

"When you said that, it really got me interested in clothes in a way that I have never been before. And – I think you will agree – my wallet was also swayed. But what you're telling me to do is just the opposite, isn't it?"

"Yes, yes, so I was right – you don't have to go on about it."

"You say I'm too pre-Lady Chatterley. I say the opposite. I'm not the child of Marilyn Monroe. She was the last in her line. I'm the child of liberated hippies. Naked liberated hippies. The taboos, the barriers and all the rest of it have all been kicked down in so many different ways, but it was the taboos and barriers that created the meaning. Now, there's nothing. There's just a well-toned man doing the physiological equivalent to construction work on a woman with more or less prosthetic body parts. I don't want to be that man."

Alice sighed.

"Now there's an image to consider."

She examined me for a moment.

"Do you know, if I were to imagine you in some contorted

sexual adventure it would be in odd ways. There's something quite ... how can I say? ... gangling about you. I somehow want to picture you with a very fat women who would more or less smother you in folds of blubber."

"Lovely," I said.

"Or perhaps you might clutch your arms around a little toy-like lady with a shaved head and a high-pitched voice, clinging on to her like tendrils of creeping ivy."

"Perhaps."

"Or perhaps not? Is that what you are saying? You don't much care for coitus, then? Coitus non-eventus, is it? Interesting."

"Hmmm," I mumbled, trying to think of a way to change the conversation. But Alice was tucking into large mouthfuls of pleasure.

"No sex for you. Well, it's a perspective. What must it be like to be fornication free? None of that rubbing, sweating, cuddling ... trying desperately not to fart. It must leave room for a lot of time to think."

"Maybe."

"I wonder why."

She studied me again, with the same surgical squint.

"A bad experience, perhaps? Easily intimidated by the sight of boobies? What can it be? I know, what about something more psychological."

She examined me closely. Her eyes ran across the surface of my face full of restrained greed. It looked like she was trying to read my mind, as she organised her own comments into orderly queues.

"How about this? Perhaps you feel some kind of ..." she hesitated, still unsure about whether to spit out the word, "...repulsion."

"Repulsion?"

"It happens."

"I don't know about that," I said, feeling more and more uncomfortable.

"It repulses you because you can't see any meaning in the act. Or – more likely – you can't see any meaning in the act because it repulses you."

"It doesn't repulse me."

"It doesn't put you at ease though – I mean, look at you now!"

"That I don't feel comfortable talking about my sexual predilections – or lack of them – with a woman twice my age who I only met for the first time yesterday, is hardly a sign of repression."

"But maybe that's just your trouble ..."

"... who says I'm troubled? ..."

"... some men make far too much out of it all. You need to get to a point where you feel at ease ... I remember with one man I knew feeling totally liberated when he asked me to masturbate in front ..."

" ... Please," I interrupted, "I'd rather not hear about this."

Her mouth remained open, frozen in the act of speech. In less than a second, she looked visibly offended.

She closed her mouth and drank from her glass of wine.

"Okay," she said.

I felt guilty.

"Sorry," I said.

Alice returned with a snap of aggression.

"You're distracting me," she said frowning. "I was letting myself get carried away. And this isn't helping. We aren't making progress. Why is none of this helping? How is it I can sit with you and talk about these things without calling to mind even a trace of my memory? And how is it – it's just ridiculous – how is it that we can recall all those scenes, word for word, without any effort? How can that happen? How can it? It's just ... ridiculous."

"I don't know," I said.

"And why does this not bother you? Why does it bother me, but it doesn't bother you? That's not right. That's not reasonable. This thing ... it's toying with us. We are its playthings! I hate that. I hate it! Why do you not hate it?"

In exasperation, she dropped her arm to the table, accidentally catching the end of her fork. This catapulted the fork to her left and hit the man next to us, squarely on the side of his face. The man let out a cry of alarm.

Alice apologised, reaching across the distance between us as concerned patrons of the restaurant turned, once again, in response to the cry. Alice continued to apologise, and offered to dab the side of his face with her napkin, but the man brushed her away. He stood up.

He turned to address Alice in an orderly way, which contained his sense of purpose. I couldn't fully understand what the man said, though it began with 'Madame ...' and his general manner made it clear that he was ready to attack. The man was well-dressed and groomed. It flowed from his nature. I could smell his aftershave.

He spoke to Alice for something like a minute, standing quite still, as he addressed her directly. His eyes looked for some kind of formal territory in the short distance between them, and his composure and confidence suggested that his mind, acting on a code of conduct, held everything in his immediate vicinity in an orderly fashion.

I couldn't tell what the man was saying, but I could tell that he was annoying her. From outward contrition, she began to shuffle uncomfortably. Her impatience and anger began to mount.

Looked at superficially, I admired something about the man. In one sense, it didn't matter what he was saying. His thoughts, the values that had motivated his rebuke, were held powerfully, and had created for him a sense of propriety, visible to anyone who cared to look. Whatever its nature, the man began from personal territory he had cultivated over time, and which he was prepared to defend proudly, maybe even against the odds.

Alice tried hard to control her outrage, but it was peeping out of her frame. If someone were to poke one of her cheeks with a piece of sharp cutlery, she might have bled bile. Before long, it just became too much for her.

She turned to confront the offender. Her head whipped swiftly into the face of the man. She said a few sharp words. It was intriguing to see how language could be deployed so quickly and to a violent purpose. The man hit back with something, and after a few rounds of scatter fire on both sides, Alice abandoned conventional warfare.

She fell short of hitting him, but she screamed, at a pitch and volume I have never heard before, waving her arms, her head lolling about on her neck, like it might break free and start biting the man about the face.

I stood up on the impulse that I should do something; but since I didn't understand what was going on, this quickly seemed futile. The man was unruffled by the display of claws and teeth. He stayed still, in more or less the same position, eyes fixed with the same cool sense of an objective. He managed to say one or two things, always cut short, and always without raising his voice too much.

The most that I could see in this very public fracas were the personalities on display. The man was the calm, collected strategist with a conservative but clear set of goals; Alice was a screeching and maniacal banshee, who, to caricature, had stripped off her clothes and was running around all arms and legs while shouting obscenities.

Not surprisingly, all the eyes of the restaurant were on us once more. In the few glances I cast around, I noticed some of the clientele looking at me directly. For some reason, I found this strange.

Someone in a position of authority – the manager, head chef or something similar – soon appeared. He blockaded the space between the two patrons of his establishment with his arm. At the same time, he gabbled through a neutral and fair line of judgement, most of which was clearly directed at Alice. He too began many of his sentences with the word 'Madame ...'.

It soon became clear that we were being asked to leave.

His spare arm pointed forcefully and unambiguously at the exit.

"Is he asking us to leave?" I asked stupidly.

We walked in silence. Alice was still fuming. I didn't want to risk a word. She would calm down in good time. She muttered something in French, which sounded like a residual insult.

"Well, don't you want to know what happened?" she asked sharply.

I asked her what it was all about.

"He told me that I was not behaving appropriately. Which is fine, you know. Nobody likes a fork in the face. But that wasn't what he meant. He meant the way I was behaving in general. Speaking loudly and so forth. Even that – you know, fine, I can live with that. Some people want a little more tranquillity while they are eating. I mean it's not a fucking library but, all the same, that's fine with me. Someone tells you to lower your voice in a restaurant, I would do as they ask. Well, perhaps. But it wasn't even that. This wasn't what bothered him. Do you know what really bothered him?"

"What was that?"

"Do you know what he said?"

"What did he say?"

"The fucking ... do you know ... he said I was not behaving appropriately for my sex."

"Blimey," I said, not really sure what to say.

If I am honest, my first reaction to this wasn't shock or moral outrage, but simply that this seemed to fit with my preconceptions about the man's character. So really I wasn't surprised at all.

"I mean," continued Alice, "as if had I been a man it would have been okay to send forks flying about the tables and speak boisterously."

Alice swung out her arms as she spoke, like she was trying to repel something.

"...I just want to fucking ... punch ..."

She sat down. Or collapsed from within. Her hair fell forward; she pulled up her legs and wrapped her arms around them. Her body shuddered. She began to cry.

This was not the sort of urbane Parisian evening full of light but meaningful conversation and continental cuisine I had envisaged. And I never expected this of Alice. I never thought I would see her cry.

It took me a moment to compose myself. For a time, I just stood there with my arms dwindling at my side, unsure what to do. Then I sat down beside her. I placed one of my arms around her. I didn't think this would meet with any response, but to my surprise she unfastened her arms from around her legs, and clung onto me.

I could see the tears in her eyes, and the eroded pattern they had left behind. She was breathing heavily, and though she didn't say anything at this point, I picked up a terrible sense of panic, a transmission of imploded or imploding adult human being. She wanted me to hold her. So I held her.

For a long time Alice clearly didn't want to speak. We just stayed as we were, looking slightly messy, maybe even like a couple of homeless drunks.

TOURISM

I escorted Alice home. She objected, telling me that it would take me in the opposite direction to my hotel and that this wasn't the 1950s, so I didn't need to offer her my elbow.

After I watched her wander into her building, I walked back through the city. I stopped at a large bistro in the city centre and ordered a beer. There were still plenty of people out and about. I even wished I had brought my book with me.

It was pleasant to watch and listen. Chatter and laughter came from small groups huddled around small café tables. There were several couples who all seemed to behave in the same way; they would sit in silence, as their eyes prowled around the city, anywhere but the immediate vicinity of their other half – as though their duality was something larger than their short-term intention – and then, occasionally, catch each other's eye over a few carefully chosen, sometimes warm, sometimes comical, words.

There were even a few people like me, though they were

mainly older, and mostly male. They would sit on their own at a table, marking their territory with a packet of cigarettes or newspaper, and sink into a position of settled observation. It struck me that some people might see this old-mannish habit of sitting on your own as a little indecent, a potential intrusion on the privacy of others, or a third cousin to prurient peeping. But, in another way, there was something more genteel and civilised about it. There must be lots of older men with reinforced habits who took a simple pleasure in this kind of activity (or inactivity).

I had the same sense of well-being I had come across the night before when Alice left me in the company of her students. I was wrapped up in a scene, but protected from it. When the table next to me roared with laughter, I almost laughed too, without knowing at what. I had the potential to become a barrel-bellied, jovial drunk, a sort of animated piece of furniture.

In reality, I was more reserved. My eyes fell and my heart raced with any suggestion that someone might try to joke with me. Luckily I maintained my distance.

And I preferred it this way. If I thought about the scant number of occasions in which I had tried to speak to strangers, they only brought with them an inward wince of pain at the memory.

This made me think about some of the things I had been talking about with Alice; and it made me think of my daubed awkwardness in general.

I only stayed in the bistro for two drinks, and then I trundled out into the street. I made my way, as I remember, up through Les Halles. I had a feeling that I was slightly lost. This didn't bother me. I even felt cheerfully indifferent about it, confident that my legs were more intelligent than my intelligence.

I walked indirectly from the city centre back to my hotel. At this hour, it felt like I was walking through the faltering failure of a sound system towards silence. Shouts and assembled laughter were common enough as I escaped the streets around the bar; and I would occasionally steal upon fragments of daytime society broken into a wasted and dishevelled version of itself.

In the pod of light created by a street lamp, a small group of young professionals huddled in happiness. They talked with the freedom and alacrity which comes in the company of friends outside working hours. They glanced at me, and a couple even smiled. I saw two girls perched on a doorstep talking semi-seriously to each other; one girl let her legs stretch across the paving stones, and the other folded them away into the comfort of her body.

For a short time, I trailed a group of musicians making their way home at the end of a performance. One had strapped a guitar to his back, and the others carried the clawed hard-shell cases of performers with pedigree.

I made my way by an infirm instinct. I could not put names to most streets or places, but I half-recognised them. I identified one long thoroughfare – the Rue Montmartre – as the route back to my hotel. I was walking into a warm breeze. Several stray people, like me suspended between their home and the purpose of an evening that had dwindled into nothing, threatened to break my rule of solitariness. Three excited girls were clearly playing some sort of game. They had taken over a corner of the street, and found fun by working against the current of pedestrians. Each approached a separate individual, and tried to arrest their movement by catching them in a conversation. This division of labour looked superficially like the work of a collective operation with a goal. It made me nervous, as I was sure one of the girls would head me off, given the ratio of their number to the people on the streets. Sure enough, one girl danced up to me.

"Excusez moi," I muttered, and tried to make my way passed her.

She tried again, keeping pace with me for a few strides, and wrapping me in a whirlwind of words, none of which I understood. I smiled and kept going. She relented.

Only a couple of minutes later, and in a moment of hope, I caught sight of a dog hopping about between diverted legs and parked cars. From a distance it was hard to judge and I might have simply willed it, but through the dusk and shade, it resembled the dog I had seen earlier and which had followed us the day before. Before I could get close enough, it slipped away into a side street, lit only by the leftover light of the main street and the glow of a few un-extinguished window lights. I stopped by the entrance to the street, hoping I might just catch the trail of a tail. To my shock, a man emerged from the veil of darkness. I stepped back, and my first instinct was to turn and walk away, but, perhaps from temporary paralysis, I looked back at the man. He was slightly – only slightly – scruffy. He wore a jumper with a visible hole in the shoulder, and was naturally camouflaged by a five o'clock shadow. His face was serious and fashioned like the hard edges of an animal. This lonely boar looked out at me from his dark wood.

"I'm sor ..." I blurted before I could catch myself saying it, "... Je suis désolé."

The man raised his lips to show his teeth. This movement was mechanical and a direct response to my words. In one way, his expression only compounded the sense of menace; but it was clear that he was intending to smile. I smiled back, and walked away. His eyes followed me down the street.

It took me the next five minutes for my mind and body to settle, and in my general state of agitation, I stopped noticing the details of the street and the people on it. I knew, by now, that I no longer wanted to stop. I encouraged the feeling as an incentive to keep going, but I could tell I was starting to feel tired. My body reached ahead of me, towards sleep.

Not long after, I found myself trailing another company. I thought about sweeping into the road to overtake them; but by this time my legs were flagging, and I was happy enough not to push them any harder.

There must have been around ten of them altogether, ambling along in pairs. They were all ages. I wondered if they were a family or if they were returning from a family function. They talked and laughed, occasionally stumbled, and laughed some more. A girl several years younger than me formed the tail of the company. She humoured the pace of her companions with an easy step, drawn out in large swinging movements that somehow suggested flying by the seat of baggy trousers. She wore black jeans, and a neat black shirt. Her hair fell in a perfect descent to her shoulder blades. It took a while before she noticed me, and then she only glanced around in a way that was reckoned to confirm a suspicion. Even in that brief glance her face rounded out a lustrous sense of entertainment. Her upper lip curled over its lower sibling, and the crested points of darkness in her eyes were mischievous screens in a piece of prestidigitation. For a while, she didn't turn to look at me again, but something had changed about her slow stride, and I could tell that she was now directing her thoughts in front and behind.

The group concertinaed over a minor disturbance: a cyclist who cut across as we were about to cross the road. The tail ground into the back of the man in front of her, and I made an effort to stop in good time; but, all the same, the distance between us collapsed to a fraction of what it had been. In this temporary closeness, one of her arms swung backwards, and brushed against mine. It grabbed me, or tried to. Her thumb and one of her fingers brushed gently down my forearm, coming together quickly so that their combined movement formed a 'v' shape. Her hand clattered over my knuckles, and returned to her side. When I looked up at her face, she was preying upon me through the corners of her eyes. She leaned forward and around, in the gesture of a spiralled bow, and opened her mouth in feigned surprise and shock.

"... désolé," I heard her say quickly and sharply, and then with no other discernible facial movement, a caricaturist quickly sketched out a smile by upturning the corners of her mouth.

I wanted to speak.

Her movements and facial expressions were familiar. Her whole comportment was theatrical, and if I was not struggling to place her in a film I had seen, then it was no effort to imagine her before the eye of an auteur's camera.

She studied the distance between us. She even turned around to stare me in the face as she walked backwards. I raised my eyebrows. She mouthed some words silently, and then turned around. I smiled to myself.

We reached my hotel. I stopped at the entrance, looking a little sadly after the girl. She turned. Her mouth dropped, her disappointment overacted. Then she kinked her hips, and wagged her finger at me. I watched her turn once more, and scurry away.

Tired, I walked through the doors of my hotel.

Sunday

THE ARTISAN'S WIFE

We were seated in Rémy's sprawling front room, startled by its strange combination of elegance and disorder. He was very keen that we should understand why he had taken up his special form of street theatre. So he read at length from one of his letters:

My Dear Coumba,

The Artisan's Wife is a little-known film made in Paris in the early 1930s. The film was the first venture into 'talkies' by a community of Russian émigré filmmakers who had made silent films in exile after Lenin nationalised the Russian film industry in 1919. The film was not a commercial success; but it helped to make the name of a French actress, Lucienne De Metz, who enjoyed a brief stint of celebrity.

De Metz had grown up in an orthodox Jewish community from Galicia, and embraced the encroaching influence of a western, secular culture by running away in search of the

Paris she had seen on dated prints and postcards. She found her way into the company of immigrant artists, including the gaggle of Russian filmmakers who later cast her in the lead role of The Artisan's Wife.

By all accounts De Metz was the only decent thing about the film. It received unfavourable public comment and hardly anyone went to see it. But it was a launchpad for her subsequent and short-lived career. She appeared in a succession of successful films throughout the 1930s, taking lead roles in a number of them. There is even a photograph from 1937 of Jean Gabin with his arm around De Metz that appeared in Film Art magazine.

De Metz said later that she felt ambivalent about The Artisan's Wife and her role in it. She looked back on it fondly because it launched her career in a much more successful direction; but since the film was rated poorly, in so far as it was rated at all, she did not want to draw too much attention to it.

By 1940 she would have been happy to remove it from the cinematic archive altogether. This would have been no great feat since most of the production team had dissembled into obscurity, and the fraction of the cinema-going public who could remember it, however vaguely, generally wished they couldn't.

The film's plot was appealing enough to attract its backers, but failed to strike a chord, even among the sections of Parisian society swayed by the romance of Russia and its patched chronicle of mysteries. The attempts at humour were lost in translation and muted by the dispirited mood of the artistic diaspora who had made it.

De Metz played a Russian countess chased into exile by the circumstances of the October revolution, but pursued by a sociopathic ideologue bent on witnessing the culmination of dialectical materialism in the state-sponsored 're-education' of his prey. To evade detection, De Metz is forced into reduced circumstances and reaches an agreement to play the fictitious wife of a misanthropic watchmaker descended from outcast Huguenots. Through a recursive twist in the plot, her pursuer swinishly assumes the guise of a Russian landowner surviving on the pocketful of roubles he could stuff into his svita before fleeing to the rococo luxury of Western Europe.

The story aimed to satirise playfully the hypocrisy and human absurdity of a society turned on its head by the theory of proletarian revolution. Afraid this might tax the interest of a western audience, the filmmakers, in a subtle celebration of cinematic trickery and the fickle nature of identity in times of social upheaval, worked into the story a romance between the watchmaker and his 'wife'. By the end of the film they assume the outward appearance of their marriage for real and elope to England to escape their assailant.

The film helped De Metz's career because she was especially well-suited to the title role, except she was playing out her own fortunes in reverse. She had come from an unremarkable background and found her way into the eye of the camera. This meant she could lend herself to the guises required by the story naturally. What is more, critics looking for something to salvage, found it in her portrayal of a Russian noblewoman. No other actress they had seen on screen had managed to convey the same kind of 'grace and fiery passion'. So much so that this film was, more than anything else, a study in the unrustled flow of her movements between cheap and unconvincing scenery.

The critics almost man-handled her through their comments, passing her around like a prize possession worthy even of trans-Atlantic attention. But the early momentum in De Metz' career tried to peak at an inauspicious time for Jewish actresses in Europe. Between 1939 and 1940 friends implored her to leave for America, but she simply didn't believe some of the hysterical warnings she heard. By autumn 1940, her career was over, and she was quickly forced to think about her survival.

After the war – in the late 1950s – she recalled her former life as an actress, movie star, and the importance of The Artisan's Wife to her career, but also the role it had played more broadly in her life. She talked quite candidly, though in private, about her experiences, her eventual marriage and escape to England.

Given the hype around her before the war, some people who knew her wondered why she hadn't tried to pursue acting either in England or America, during or after the war. She would often turn the same look on the questioner. By this time, some of her glamour had faded, but she retained the effortless allure of her screen persona. Her instinct was somehow tempered.

Her extended answer to the question began with her

childhood. As a child, and particularly growing up as a young woman, she desperately wanted to forget or escape her background. At this time, being Jewish was the basis for exclusion and, from some quarters, persecution. She had experienced anti-Semitism first-hand as a child, but the issue, she believed, was much deeper than the sense of righteous indignation or heightened self-awareness occasioned by the shrill cry of unthinking social judgement. The firmly held beliefs of the community in which she had grown up could simply not find enough air with which to breathe.

They called it the Judenfrage, the 'Jewish Question', and it had, indirectly or directly, shaped many of her actions and decisions. It was a question that had become especially fraught with tension as she grew up, by wave after wave of East European Jews arriving in Western Europe following the Russian pogroms. The 'tension' came from the clash of culture and identity between secular society, and the gnarled roots of Hasidic tradition. For many who stood in the middle, the force of this conflict tore them apart.

For a young woman the scent of hedonism was too overpowering to resist. Fighting the baggage of ritual, the direction of travel was irresistible. Partly, she wanted the liberated life that the world of the western metropolis afforded: the cafés, the trams and omnibuses, the parks, the boutiques and the theatres. Partly, she wanted the glamour that this world seemed to enfold upon itself, and which was, in her eyes, concentrated in the theatre and the arts.

But looking back at a later time in her life, she could see other interests. So many people of her generation had been drawn to the Yiddish theatre, and found their way into the spectacle of the stage and screen through this route. Was this, she wondered, any more than a vibrant tradition within the Jewish community? Was the danger of the Jewish Question that the conflict of identities threatened no identity and the search for a costume through which to make only a passing appearance in the world?

At the height of her involvement in the theatre, and later the cinema, she was faintly aware of these questions, discussed heatedly by intellectuals, defenders of the faith, and the movement towards Zionism; but unlike these contemporaries, she saw the subject as fuel for political anger, disaffection and trouble. If identity only provided the flimsy excuse for violence, was it not better to soften it in the performance of fake identities?

The succession of statutes on Jews introduced by the Vichy Government in the second half of 1940 had clamped down around Lucienne. Her public identity became a problem. Even if she had not found the sort of fame that would have made it difficult for her to walk down the street unescorted, the authorities certainly recognised her, and had monitored and engineered the gradual waning of her star. But only when a producer screamed at her to find a way – any way – to leave the country did she act.

"Did she think this was a joke?!" he yelled. It wasn't a joke. This was a programmatic act of government. She would not end up unemployed, a little short of cash or snubbed by a few friends for whom she never much cared anyway. She would be crushed by the juggernaut of executive power. She would be administered out of existence. And she was not to cling vainly to the belief that a government could never kill someone who had caught the public's eye. They could. Not only that, they could write her out of its memory altogether.

They had not wasted any time either. They had not cut her down in full public view; but no government, however discriminatory and violent, would be quite so tactless. She had played the protagonist in many stories – did she not realise that they were fashioning the story of her ruin?

They would do it gradually. First they would prevent her from working. Audiences were not that sentimental and loyal. What would happen then? It could be anything: poison, an 'accidental' fall of some kind (people break their necks all the time).

Lucienne, though she had left it late, had heard enough. The only question to answer was: how would she act? This question gleamed with interpretation, and she was left dizzy with possibilities and suggestions, one as daring and ridiculous as the next. How well could she swim? Did she know how to fly a plane? How many languages could she speak? Had she ever fired a gun? And could she find a secret place to keep the cyanide?

To her, the only route to escape was the route she had always followed; the only route she could see clearly, and with which she felt comfortable, was the people she had played on screen. The question 'how would she act?' was really just another version of the Judenfrage, to which she had already responded many years ago; only now, under cross-examination, the questioner looked her squarely in the face. To respond in any other way implied a concession to the values of the new government. They may have made her professional pursuit of escapism impossible, but that did not mean that escapism was not a possible route to escape.

The more she calculated her options, the more it looked like the only logical way to survive. To accept the pragmatic peril of her predicament and devise a scheme with enough legerdemain to outwit the authorities was naïve and played into the enclosed world in which they wanted her to wither away. They knew exactly who she was; they even had a file that recorded her identity and made it official. She could only beat them by rejecting the identity, and with it the version of reality they had created. She needed a rival view of things that restated the act of dissimulation and disguise.

And once she reached this conclusion, the details of her plan began to fall into place. The parallels with the story of the The Artisan's Wife were too obvious to ignore, and since this was the film that brought her success, it seemed fitting that it should turn her life in a new direction. She could also see the risks. If this idea was obvious to her, then it might also be obvious to those who were trying to trap her. Would they be that familiar with her portfolio of work? The Artisan's Wife was, of all her films, the least well-remembered, so there was a good chance they would not see the connection. To pursue the idea would, nevertheless, require nerve and a certain amount of cheek.

It would be easy enough to do, wouldn't it? She put this question to one of her trusted friends to judge their reaction. She still had the wardrobe she had worn for the part.

She could look like the wife of a watchmaker tomorrow, without going to any trouble. Her friend worked in the film industry, so was naturally keen on the idea; but even over-excited by their childish imagination, they could not escape the shadow of the new regime and the practical difficulties she would face.

"It's not enough just to look like someone," her friend told her.

Lucienne was jolted with fear by these words. They made her idea sound like a childish answer to an adult's problem. For a brief moment she wanted to dismiss the whole scheme as absurd. Then she thought again.

"Yes. It is," she replied.

And thereafter they just turned their attention to the details of her disguise.

For the plan to work, she needed to find a cantankerous Huguenot watchmaker with connections across the channel; at least, she needed to find someone willing to play this role. And to make either of the roles convincing, she would need documents, passports, official paperwork. This meant clandestine meetings with the self-organising community of the resistance.

In her situation, and knowing many people in her line of work who made a scarcely kept secret of their enmity towards Pétain and his new government, she already had some idea how to go about it. The hard part was dissuading them of the risk she posed to their operations. She had been a well-known actress, they said. That meant officials would certainly know about her, and might even be monitoring her movement. In time, as the tentacles of the new government took hold, she would be an obvious target. Time might just be on their side if they acted soon, but it was no small risk. Why had she left it this late to think about moving?

Entering into the spirit of their concerns she negotiated with her plan. It was no secret that the resistance were helping allied soldiers, POWs, and increasingly, airmen to escape the country. So her idea was simple: would it not make it easier to smuggle out one of these men if they were disguised as a married watchmaker? After due consideration, they said they liked the idea, but were still concerned that, even in disguise, she would turn too many heads!

Her case suited the plight of an English officer – Lieutenant Patrick Fielding – from the East Surrey Regiment of the British Expeditionary Force who had been badly injured in the preamble to Dunkirk. Looked after by a farmer, he had been handed over to the resistance, who had wanted to ferry him south to Marseilles using the emerging Pat O' Leary Line but they soon realised that, in the short term, his injuries would prevent the journey. He had a broken right leg, shattered foot, and hair singed on one side.

After a skirmish, he had hobbled or, more likely, crawled (he could not remember which) into a field, and collapsed unconscious, where he was later found. This meant he needed medical attention and a period of recuperation. The resistance moved him about and he was sucked into several safe houses on the edge of Paris. His French had been a little rusty. Well enough recovered to believe he could follow the Pat Line, he was now eager to do so, even though he could still scarcely walk properly.

"Is injury within the scope of your film?" they asked Lucienne.

"It was not in the original scenario," she replied. "But I have always believed in artistic licence."

She first met her Mari in some old offices in the heart of Paris that had been used at one time by a small publishing house. He sat in a very plush-looking chair with gilt edges, wearing a navy suit, esquire jacket and white shirt. He sandwiched a large walking stick between his right arm and leg.

"You are an actress?" he asked in French.

"Yes," she replied.

"I must say it is rather an odd fix," he continued, this time in English.

Her main concern had always been that he would look too obviously English; and that someone who looked like a previously famous Jewish actress, arms hooked up to an English-looking man with a limp would be no kind of disguise at all. In his company, she was reassured. He did not look French, just 'a little different'.

She shook him by the hand, and caught herself in the act of these calculations. She realised swiftly that she would need to do more than this; she would need to appear to show him some affection. Would this be difficult? Could she appear to love this man? She thought so. Actresses were always falling in love with their co-stars.

They spent several weeks preparing. The threat of a sudden departure, if circumstances were favourable, hung over them. In this time, they got to know each other a little. They planned their journey; who they might meet, who could be trusted, what they needed to say, their eventual route through Spain.

She told him their story. She even gave him a copy of the original screenplay, and asked him to memorise lines.

His manner was peculiarly formal, in ways that worked incongruously through a romance language. This, she guessed, was the outward sign of English stoicism. Concerned, but quietly amused, she encouraged him to temper it as a detectable sign of his Englishness. In reply, he said something that surprised her. He said he thought he could detect the trace of a foreign tongue in her accent. She smiled.

"I suppose that is why we find ourselves thrown together like this. And that is why we need our story. Remember you are a miserable French watchmaker descended from outcast Protestants."

"And who are you again? It's all so complicated!"

They spent afternoons in different parts of the city, mingling with the rest of the civilian population, perfecting their ease in each other's company. They read from different sections of the script: outside a church near the Pont d'Austerlitz, at the Gare de Lyons, and on the banks of the Seine.

She knew that their romance and eventual marriage began in these early meetings under the nose of occupying German soldiers. She could recall, in particular, several lines from their script. They were the countess' words, spoken at a point of rapprochement towards the end of the story. The countess looked at the watchmaker and said:

"It is only in what I say, tainted with all its disguises and falsehoods, that you will ever find anything. If you will not put your arms around this marionette, then, in different ways, the elements will sweep us away."

"It is an unusual reckoning," the watchmaker replied.

"Yes," said the countess.

Their escape began a few days later. They reached England, not without incident, by summer 1941. Three years later they married.

The events of her escape from Paris led Lucienne to reconsider the life she had led before the war. She had reached stardom more by instinct than design, and on reflection it made her uncomfortable. Running away into the hedonism of the twenties and thirties looked like a convenient denial of the question asked about Jewish identity rather than an attempt at an answer. That was not all; it left the question open to an insidious answer. Denial of her identity was, on reflection, complicit with the monster from which it wanted to hide.

This was the real significance, in her mind, of the The Artisan's Wife. The irony was, of course, that the star persona she fleetingly became was, in the end, no more substantial than the obscurity and anonymity from which she had emerged. The 'real' name it helped to make was the name she borrowed from the film, which helped her to survive, and through which she discovered her husband and a new lease of life. This 'real' name just happened to be fake.

A film made by depressed Russians with an elaborate

plot and a covert theme of political satire (lost on most members of the public who were just looking for a cheap thrill and a bit of romance), had given her the materials and details with which to construct a life for herself that was neither threatened by alienation and extinction nor visible only through the projections on a screen. Out of the silence to which she had, in different ways, been confined, it gave her a new form, and through it, the means to speak for the first time.

This was the reason she did not want to return to her life as an actress, because such a return would imply something missing, and which, until the crisis of the 1940s, had been missing. It was something that for many other people caught up in the war – Jewish or not – had simply been snuffed out. But The Artisan's Wife had given her clothes in which to walk around with some measure of dignity; and acutely aware how threadbare they were, she was not about to let them slip away.

The life she had invented, using the imaginary character from The Artisan's Wife, had brought her love, family and a home. Through this reinvention, the past, its memories, customs and ghosts, could at least find some entry into the world.

Postscript: Lucienne De Metz is a little-known and mostly forgotten footnote in the history of cinema. I only happen to know her story because, as a young man in the 1950s, I was fortunate enough to meet her. The story made an impression on me, and at times, I even thought about writing it up; but it struck me that I would never really do it justice, and, in any case, I sensed that this was not something Lucienne would have wanted. In time my own life took its course and, partially forgotten, I filed the story away.

It was only much later when I first met you that I dredged it up. At this time, I was especially ungainly and ungraceful, even diffident. We had been dating a little while, and I knew where these dates were leading. I badly wanted to find a way of crossing the ground between us. Our evenings, I remember, would often end in awkward silences, and occasionally – in the cinema, for example – you would turn your head towards mine, and I would only stare more furiously at the screen.

It is strange that this kind of eagerness to take you in my arms could become an obstacle; and stranger still that the only way I could find to overcome it was to enact it in the role of someone else. Strange as this seems, when the idea came to me, it made perfect sense, and I knew it was the only thing I could do. I can also still remember how easy it was to enact our romance through the patterns carved out by others. I think you knew this at the time – in fact I think we talked about it – but when I held you for the first time and we kissed there was nothing fake about it. We had just found a form that answered to our appeal for each other's attention. This, as I understand it, is exactly what Lucienne De Metz found in the same story. And just as it shaped a new identity and meaning for her, it did the same for the two of us.

This meant I had found a use for the story; a use, I

thought, of which Lucienne would have approved. So when you died I knew that I should do something with her story. Just as The Artisan's Wife had helped her and also helped me, surely it would be able to help others? And by helping others, I would witness our own connection re-lived in many different ways. So, in one way or another, I have managed to find people who are willing to participate in this little piece of theatre. Many of them, naturally enough, think it is very strange at first, but most of them – in fact almost all of them – manage to make it their own and renew, or discover, some kind of union.

The idea is quite simple: if a story like this can resolve the actors to an end that has some meaning and value (in the face of human behaviour that reduces life to a pulp) what good is it if it serves no purpose?

All my love
Rémy

PARANOIA

The day had begun early. Far too early for a holiday, I thought. I had been woken up at seven thirty in the morning by reception. A lady was here to see me. I knew it would be Alice, but reception had insisted that I go down to meet her. So I had thrown on some clothes, trundled down the stairs, collected her, climbed back up the stairs, and held an unproductive argument about this sort of unorthodox behaviour, while I suffered a feeling of being unwashed and sticky with sleep.

We had agreed to meet Rémy that morning at his apartment. I had realised through a thin veil of reality, that we had not agreed a time; but only that we would see him at some point in the morning. Alice had obviously thought that this was a respectable and suitable time. I hadn't.

I had moved about my hotel room like a creature so large it is forced to move slowly, stumbling intermittently on words spoken by either one of us. After some subtle goading and maidenly manipulation, Alice had directed me into the bathroom, where I had washed, and re-dressed. Then we had bundled into her car, and made our way to Rémy's.

"He lives in Neuilly," Alice had said as we drove.

"Oh," I had replied.

"Neuilly is one of the richest suburbs of Paris," she had explained. "It's where the bourgeoisie live."

"Oh," I had said again, this time with more surprise.

Rémy, it seemed, had more money than his unclean appearance would allow. As we drove, I had begun to wonder what might await us.

The apartment was certainly plush and decorous. It bore out vestiges of its owner's slovenly appearance, but most of the interior was so effortlessly marked by good taste that even using a description like 'tastefully chaotic' was misleading. The chaos was superimposed on a pedigree of refinement and sophistication. Books, folders, papers had strayed from their intended place to serve some practical purpose, and never quite found their way back. A set of simple, almost incomplete, drawings or sketches by the same artist hung on the walls in each room, placed carefully, even thoughtfully, so they might solicit attention without contrasting crudely with the colour of the walls and the coving.

"Who was this man?" I had thought when I entered the apartment.

The question was well-placed, since Rémy spent most of our visit providing the answer.

After the scene at the Gare de Lyons the day before, he had insisted repeatedly that we should visit him in his apartment. It was very important, he said. Something was going on that he didn't understand and we were part of it. It was very exciting, but he wanted to explore it all with us in more detail.

Before we began he had supplied us with strong coffee and a simple white cheese served with honey. This was, by this stage, very welcome. Alice preferred not to eat, and Rémy said he had already breakfasted, so for ten minutes they watched me as I took pleasure in my first experience of honey-coated cheese and made appreciative noises which excited smiles from my observers.

I had started to wonder if it would be acceptable for me to dip my finger in the smeared remains of cheesy honey, when Rémy had said "I want to read you a letter." He had stepped out of the room and gone in search of the letter about Lucienne de Metz and The Artisan's Wife. In his absence, and before the explanation began, I could feel myself being easily seduced by the life that Rémy led: the beautiful apartment, the books, the quiet esoteric routine, the honey and cheese. I had leaned back in my chair in a way that must have suggested the life of a privileged pig smugly settled into his comfortable existence yet unjustly disdainful of anyone who had not quite attained to it. Was this true? Would I become an aristocratic tyrant if this kind of fortune landed in my lap? Would I employ obsequious servants to form the object of psychological abuse? Would I spend my days draped in a silk dressing gown as I paid for expensive prostitutes to sing German lieder naked at the grand piano? Or was this just the honey and cheese talking?

Before Rémy had started to read his letter out loud, he

had explained that it was written to his wife, after she had past away.

"**After** she had past away?" Alice had exclaimed a little too loudly.

"I will explain how it has come to pass that I write letters to my dead wife. Really I don't think it is so strange, or for that matter unusual, as the tone of your question suggests. But for now, it's not directly relevant. I begin the letter 'My Dear Coumba'. It is enough to say that Coumba was my wife and that she died in the early 1990s. Of cancer. But Coumba is not the subject of the letter, as you will see."

Then he had plunged into the letter, all the while standing before us, like he was delivering a public lecture or 'performing' a public reading.

I soon became caught up in the details of his letter as its relevance to us became clear, but as the pieces were falling into place I couldn't stop my mind wondering about his wife. Rémy was a very tall, angular man, and, for a reason I didn't know, I wanted to envisage his wife as smaller and rounder. She would be half his height. He would tower over her so that the distribution of height in the room was unbalanced and created creatures out of a mythical fairy tale recast in the fabrics, interior design and social space of the modern world.

I tried to muster my concentration, and restrain the needless multiplication of entities, but odd images kept making unprompted appearances in my head: the eyes of his wife sticking out above the dashboard of a car, as Rémy's head more or less went through the roof.

By the time he had finished reading his letter, my mind had filled with many more purposeful and pressing thoughts and questions. Alice was obviously brimming with the same impatient curiosity, and, without giving Rémy much pause for thought or breath, she began firing questions, picking on and deconstructing the details of his letter, and trying to tie it back to him and us.

It took a long time for everything to unravel. Our visit lasted over four hours.

"I will answer all your questions," said Rémy, raising his voice a little over the rising din, "but you must allow me to keep speaking for a while. You can see from the letter I have just read you where the story I enact with my clients comes from. That is not unusual. I have been doing it for years. But what happened yesterday with you two was, without question, unusual. I have experienced something like it, but nothing quite like it. And from some of the things you have said already, I can see that it was an abnormal experience for you too."

"Abnormal?" Alice stuttered, "that hardly ..."

"... just a minute, Madame," Rémy interrupted. "Before you go on to tell me, I would like to guess what you are about to say. Will you allow me to guess?"

"Very well."

"Everything you have spoken to each other through the two scenes you have enacted these last two days you knew already, didn't you? It was a memory. You didn't know where they came from, but the words were in your mouth. Am I right?"

"Yes," I said before Alice could reply, "but how did you know?" I asked.

A sickening pit of paranoia was swelling up inside me.

"Because the same thing was happening to me," he replied directly. "I knew I had seen you before when we met for the first time on Friday, but I was not sure where. And I mean, who knows? I see thousands of tourists throughout the year; it seemed quite likely to me that I had chanced upon you briefly at some point in the past. But yesterday, this all changed outside the Gare de Lyons. As I became part of the scene ... I had nothing to say, I know, but nevertheless, when I appeared in the guise of the Russian assassin, I knew instinctively, and without thinking, exactly what to do. Given the letter I have just read to you, that might not seem so unusual. I know the story inside out, after all. But not in that particular way. And I knew exactly what each of you were going to say. Every couple says different things when they put words into the scene, but your words ... I knew them. And I knew you. I knew that the memory I had not quite placed the day before, had come ... this is the crazy part, no? ... it had come from the day after."

Alice and I were silenced.

"I can tell from your silence, that we all experienced the same thing. Don't you think this is fascinating?" He paused for a moment. "Yesterday you told me that you don't know each other. That's right, isn't it?"

"That's right," I replied.

"We met for the first time on Friday," said Alice.

Rémy spent some moments thinking things over, and we

all tried hard to relax into this unnatural meeting of minds.

"I think I have an explanation of sorts," said Rémy eventually. "But you might not accept it. And you must bear with me.

'As I have already said in my letter to Coumba, I first remembered the story when I was trying to overcome my diffidence with her. It provided a way to make the final connection we had both wanted. But, as I also said, my wife is now dead, and after her death the story became a way to remember her. Except, by doing so, it led me to question which came first: my wife or the story. And, self-evidently, the story came first."

His full name was Rémy Beauchene. He was the only son in a wealthy family of industrial engineers from Normandy. Rémy grew up in a secluded estate on the Normandy coast. He excelled in most things from an early age. He read Latin and Greek, and by his late teens was fluent in English, German and Italian. He mastered mathematics, the natural sciences, philosophy, history, literature. This intelligence brought him success. His great brain led him to the Institut d'étude politiques de Paris. Alice explained to me that the prestigious 'Sciences Po' was among the most famous of all the grand écoles and had served the preferment of many leading dignitaries, politicians, diplomats, even Presidents, at the very heart of France's political elite. From there, like many of his high-achieving contemporaries, he graduated to the École nationale d'administration, and subsequently began a career as a high-ranking civil servant destined to play a formative role in the affairs of state.

In the early years of his career, back in the 60s and 70s, he worked for a fixed period at the Inspection générale des finances and then at France's finance ministry. In this period, he saw the tail end of the country's post-war economic expansion, the so-called 'thirty glorious years'. He was closely involved in a few final wags of the tail, working for the De Gaulle and Pompidou administrations on substantial investments in public infrastructure, the expansion of the motorways and metro network, and flooding the public coffers of the Ministry of Telecommunications.

The picture formed quickly. He was a classic member of the metropolitan elite: rich family, very clever, a product of the right schools and connected to all the right people. He was someone to whom, as I found out more about him, I wanted to defer out of sheer intellectual and social intimidation.

On paper Rémy may have looked a paragon of traditional success and achievement, but his unfolded character revealed something more unconventional. Later, Alice told me she thought he was like a plant, only one side of which received exposure to the sun, so that some leaves were more distended than others. At an early age he read widely, but in particular the literature and philosophy of the ancient world.

There were some early signs that the path prescribed for him caused some resentment, or at least a reaction. There were occasional disagreements in the family; but Rémy, it seemed, 'showed' his reaction more through odd forms of behaviour than tantrums and household fist-fights.

At social functions he would sometimes disappear from the room without telling anyone, only to be found several hours later wandering in the garden trying to identify the species and genera for all the different varieties of flora. He also enjoyed deceit and deception, particularly on social occasions. At the age of eighteen he once turned up to one of his parents' dinner parties dressed as a vagrant claiming to live off their 'Christian largesse'. Even when he became a senior civil servant there were rumours that he would sometimes walk the streets of Paris in different disguises.

Listening to him talk about it, I noticed a pattern in his 'odd' behaviour. His disguises and eccentricities looked like ways of escaping, even denying, his privileged background. Looking back, I could see the early years of his story, were almost contrived to illustrate what followed, which made me wonder, cynically, if he had embellished the truth.

Rémy met his wife on a trip to London with a delegation of officials. He met her in the lobby of his hotel. He noticed her struggling with some bags, so he offered her his help. They talked. Rémy, eventually, told her that he would rather spend an evening with a mannequin than in the company of his delegation, and since it only required her to be no less interesting than a mannequin, he asked her if she would like to have a drink with him. A lot of correspondence followed. They crossed the channel to see each other several times. And eventually they got married.

"It is very hard to explain ... and I am someone who is interested in explanations and trying to find effective ways to explain ... but it is very hard to explain ... love," he said reflectively.

The eccentricities of his character became clear when he explained that he didn't tell anyone about this relationship and marriage. Friends, family, work colleagues were all equally in the dark. He just announced, out of the blue, that he had got married to a second-generation Afro-British woman called Coumba.

Rémy seemed keen to dwell on this point as a matter of interpretation, and encouraged us to do the same.

"Some people, I believe, thought that I had calculated my marriage. They saw it as a sort of move in the dynamics of my family and the wider social strata to which they belonged – to which I still belong. To marry a black woman from a different social class, even then in the progressive spirit of the time, was controversial, especially among the older generations of my family. My father in particular. They thought, I suppose, that the marriage and the love affair was a form of reaction, or protest, against my background. I was obviously unhappy with my background, they said. That was the only way – the only way, you see – to explain it. It caused a rift with my father for many years.

'But to use someone from a less privileged background out of protest, even if only in an unconscious and unthinking way, is a very political thing to do. And how much is lost in that kind of judgement? I would say that everything is lost, wouldn't you? Especially where love is concerned."

Early on, some had expected that Rémy would go into politics, not because he inclined towards the trappings and machinations of power, but simply because he was so well-qualified to do it. But in the early stages of his career it quickly became clear that he did not have the right character for it. He did not have the competitive edge to cultivate the right people or any clear sense of who were the right people to cultivate. The machinery of government and the technical implementation of a policy, or the practical pursuit of a problem, he could understand. But to stand above all the horse trading with the power factions, lobby groups and vested interests that powered the machinery into life did not come to him naturally. He became known as a level-headed technocrat, a cool custodian of continuity and order.

"Politics does not come naturally to me. So, I am adamant, that there was more to my marriage than a study in social psychology. Politics does not even come into it."

Some people, he said, came to recognise that his relationship with Coumba was sincere, and that the way he had formed and announced the relationship to the world just reflected his unusual bent of mind. But the marriage, he was just as sure, changed the way people saw him. Not that it met with discrimination or prejudice. Most people who had moved in the same social circles as Rémy until that point, came to think that they simply did not know or understand him.

"'What else don't we know about this person?' people asked, and 'Do we really know him at all?' Some were even affronted that I had kept the romance secret, thinking that perhaps I thought they were too reactionary to give the marriage their blessing. This is the trouble. Mystery and enigma are all very well if you are a saint or an artist, or something of that sort. People almost expect it. But then, I suppose, you might ask, is it really mystery and enigma? But in more conventional walks of life, they are a blank page, with an open invitation to write whatever takes your fancy. At one level it is both disgusting and depressing: why should it matter who you marry? And yet even when those around you are determined that it should not matter, it does. The simple fact that, back then, we spent so much time talking and thinking about it – and I suppose that I should have elaborated this all at such length – is, itself, depressing. Why, you want to ask, can't people just be in love?"

From the way he told it, his marriage caused more than a few raised eyebrows. He worked with many ambitious people, he said, and it was naïve to think that people wouldn't talk, and if they saw the opportunity, exploit the circumstance. In a half-ironic way, some younger members of his staff started to refer to him as 'the underground man'. This was harmless enough, but, Rémy thought it undermined his credentials as a fonctionnaire (even if he recognised its ring of truth).

"Some people gossiped. Some people intrigued. I cared less about that. Some of my friends thought I should have cared more about it, especially given how things turned out. Some people I knew and respected reacted in a different way. I think I must have seemed less like someone familiar in their eyes. I was someone with secrets. I was clearly someone who was not entirely open and honest with his friends. Did this imply a judgement, they thought? 'Does he not trust us?' they asked. 'Or are his outward appearances cultivated to suit the privileged office he holds?' It, in other words, eroded the trust they had placed in me.

'And I think, if I am honest, they were right to react in that way. It is a natural reaction. If you aren't at least a large part of what you appear to be, then it must be upsetting for those around you and they are entitled to treat you with more caution. And, in a different kind of way, my marriage exposed uncomfortable truths that I was not willing to face. I grew up in an environment that treated me very well; it gave me the best possible education and connections; it went to every possible length to support the particular path I had chosen (or which had been laid out for me). But I have always felt that the path and the education came first. They came first and I came second. Now since I am not a very resilient personality, I acquiesced (not unhappily) and I played the part I was meant to play. But things have a way of not working out when you do that.

'And that's what I am getting at: this is what happened when I met Coumba. It drew to the fore parts of my personality that I didn't know existed and it made me happy in ways that I never thought possible. This was not easy to reconcile with the person I had become, so I failed to cope with it by keeping quiet.

'I am sorry if this seems like a rather long way round to the purpose of our meeting this morning, but I hope that you will begin to glimpse from everything I have said that my wife was important to me. More important than I can really say. And this is why I turned back to the story when she died. I started by just writing to her, but re-enacting the story of The Artisan's Wife took it one stage further; it made it more real. And the more I repeated the story with couples drawn from the streets of Paris, the more I came to realise that the thing I was trying to recall was deeper than my relationship with Coumba. My marriage, it seems to me, served the very same thing that the story safeguards. It worked towards it, almost under its employment."

Rémy's wife died at the wrong time. They caught the cancer late, and she died within six months of diagnosis, in late 1993. Towards the end of the 1980s and in the early 1990s, Rémy had overseen a number of high-profile public contracts with industry. Throughout the period leading up to his wife's death, and for a while after, a succession of stories broke in the media about misconduct of public procurement and so-called 'pantouflage', or the cosy relationship between senior ranks of the civil service and industry. Given his role, Rémy was one of the individuals implicated in these stories. A subsequent investigation exonerated him, but the dovetailing of these two events – his wife's death and the public allegations of professional misconduct – weakened his position.

Rémy was often known to be oblique and taciturn, but these events lent this side of his character new force. His staff noted that he would carry out all his duties as before, even looking to create meetings and opportunities where previously they had not existed. But he undertook this work in a more perfunctory way, as though he had simply abandoned himself to the mechanics of administration. Where previously he had tolerated social occasions, albeit in an aloof way, now he plotted his way around them, evading informal contact with anyone.

And, discreetly, between the gaps of this routine, some of the peccadilloes rumoured about his private life began to surface. His secretarial staff began to notice it most of all. On several occasions his secretary walked into his office to find him staring blankly across the room at the wall. She spoke to him, but no matter what she said, he would not respond. Little abnormalities like this quickly circulated around his office and got back to his peers. One of his closest colleagues had noticed that, since the death of his wife, he would often retreat for long lunch hours alone. With mounting concern, he took it upon himself to follow Rémy. From a distance, he followed him into the Bercy gardens, where he watched this esteemed and well-respected dignitary of French officialdom walk up and down over the same spot for an hour and a half.

These irregularities fuelled hearsay and speculation. There was talk about even stranger behaviour: that he had been seen walking the streets late at night dressed as a woman, that he had got so drunk one evening he fell in the river, that he had, on more than one occasion, tried to kill himself. Rémy made it quite clear that none of these rumours were true, and that many of them were positively invented by some key senior members of the political establishment who felt there was something to be gained by shuffling the decks of senior officials.

Some of his friends within the service had wanted simply to offer him a leave of grace in view of the difficult events with which he was coming to terms. But someone made representations at the highest level within his department. He was approached with a generous superannuation. Rémy hinted that he had been threatened with further 'revelations' about his alleged entanglements with business. Did he wish to damage his personal reputation any further? Or that of the government? He was forced, finally, to recognise the political circumstance in which he found himself, and, with no stomach for a fight that fashioned weapons from an economical view of the truth, he accepted the offer of early retirement. The door closed on his career quickly, quietly and discreetly.

Rémy became a virtual recluse, subsisting in a routine known only to himself, and locked away in the high-ceilinged rooms of his apartment. In these spaces, he started to reflect on the relationship with his wife. And then he began to write her letters.

"Things became clearer to me the more I watched other people act out the story," he said.

It interested him to see how different couples responded to the 'street theatre'. Most – as Alice and I had been – were initially wary, but as soon as they had the opportunity to find their own words and inject their own dialogue into the scenario, all were somehow taken up with it. Some discovered pathos through the scenes; for others, it all quickly turned to farce. Some were flat; for others the volume was bouffant.

I could begin to see how different couples might recreate the story in the shadow of their shared personality. More temperate versions of Alice might too easily crumble and submit to a dominant partner. More confectionary crooners than me might have made their co-stars melt. And just as some couples would discover a chapter of romance, so I could imagine the chapped cheeks of a middle-aged Danish couple determined to discover anomie and an existential crisis.

"It's strange watching the story brought to life by different people. It's always interesting just to meet new people. People are very different. And sometimes how they seem at first is not entirely consistent with the way they then play the parts. They can be very quiet, and withdrawn, but as soon as they realise they are putting on some kind of performance, a veil lifts (or descends – I am not sure which) and they become flamboyant, and charismatic. Seeing the different ways that people respond is fascinating.

'But, of course and as I have already said, my original intention was to relive the first magical moments with my wife. And in a sense, I was just treating people as puppets to indulge my desperate fantasies. Until I came to see ... I mean it's obvious really ... I came to see that I had no more claim to the story than they did. The story is not my story, after all. I just borrowed it from someone else. And they borrowed it from someone else too. And, who knows, maybe the Russian filmmakers borrowed it from somewhere. So it goes on.

'All of which, if you are in a reflective mood, might make

you think. These people are recreating my memories, while they are creating new ones of their own. But of course this means that the memory is not 'my' memory or 'their' memory. We are not talking about a set of events that happened to me and which I make other people enact. The events that the story is trying to recall precede me. In which case, is it sensible to talk of 'a memory' or a place from which all these memorable experiences begin? Did someone invent the story in an original form? Maybe, in the original, the protagonists were not a watchmaker and a countess, but a peasant and a princess, a gentlewoman and a slave, or some other expression of an elusive 'archetype'. In any case, whatever the story signifies it certainly doesn't belong to me. Even if it was very important to me.

'So my attitude has changed. I no longer want to possess the story. I want to serve it. All I want to do now is sustain it through people like you; through the complete range of eccentric human behaviour. All of which makes me wonder: what, ultimately, does it recall?"

When Rémy stopped talking for a moment, Alice and I could just notice our shared act of listening, like it was a background noise amplified by a sudden silence in the foreground. His eyes brushed over us lightly, just sensing the level of our interest and curiosity. And then he continued.

"And that question begins to open up a whole other way of thinking. What happened yesterday – well, I don't really understand it. By its nature I couldn't really understand it. It makes a mockery of us."

"You don't say," said Alice flatly.

Taking this on board, I began to see how I was not so troubled by the events of the last few days, since a general state of mockery was more or less an unspoken assumption of the way I managed to function. I began to feel something like affection for the dimly lit contents of my brain and its unpredictable use of my larynx.

"But the one thing that seems clear to me is that we can talk about everything that has happened to the two of you (and the small part I have played in that) as a memory. You might not be fully aware of it, but it is referring you to something that you already know.

'Speaking for myself, I have only ever had that sense of recovering a broader perspective in fragments and at odd moments. The closest I came to it was when I was on the verge of a breakdown shortly after my wife died.

'I have told you already how things did not go well for me in the early nineties. And the things that did not go so well happened more or less simultaneously. Have you ever noticed that? That bad things quite often happen in clusters?

'It stands to reason that I should have felt agitated in that time. A period of great strain. That's what people said, I believe. They said he is under great strain. We should reserve some sympathy for him. It is a test of his character. Will he come through it?"

"Well, he did, didn't he?" asked Alice.

"I suppose that depends in what light you look at it."

"You're telling the tale aren't you?," she added.

"I think misfortune isn't always completely unfamiliar. It's not a feral force of nature that steals entry to your inner sanctuary. It's unpleasant because it is familiar.

'In some weeks everything goes wrong. You must have had a week or a day like that. No matter what you do, things just won't go your way. When that happened to me, I always had the same thought: this seems like too much of a coincidence. It's improbable, surely! In fact it almost seems contrived. Like there must be someone who has engineered this succession of misfortunes, and disguised their plan by calling it 'bad luck'.

'The language of 'bad luck' makes these sort of experiences acceptable to common sense, and so carries with it readmission to society. Everyone can accommodate the idea of arbitrary misfortune, but the idea of a conspiracy is unhealthy and counter-intuitive. The idea of bad luck almost mildly chastises you into not dwelling on your misfortune. 'It isn't good manners to do that,' it seems to say.

'But if, like me, you like to reflect on things, then it is amazing how easily you can survey this contrivance, and turn to 'bad luck' with an inscrutable face.

'I want to just recall some very particular instances, if you will let me.

'Some years ago, shortly before my father died, I remember something that happened at the very end of a working day. The day before I received a call from my mother to tell me that father was unwell, and that they were all worried about his health. She wanted me to visit. I decided then and there that I would visit, but throughout the next day, I could not concentrate properly. I kept thinking about the strained relationship that I had with my father. So I decided, as a matter of urgency, to write him a letter. I stole a long lunchtime, and I set down everything I wanted to say: how I had always admired him, and how much I regretted our temporary falling out.

'No sooner had I finished the letter than a man, who was at that time my senior, walked into my office. He wore a peculiar expression, as though he were under instruction to interrogate me, and did not feel comfortable about it. He apologised for intruding, and then, a little hesitantly, he said 'I hear your father is unwell.' I paused, without yet feeling stunned. I told him that he was correct. 'In that case,' he said, 'I think you should visit him.' I told him that I intended to. 'Well, that's good,' he replied, somehow reassured. And then he left my office.

'To this day, I have no idea how this colleague knew how my father was unwell.

'I remember another incident. It was only brief. I was sitting in my office, at work, staring across the room, my mind half on a budget problem, and the other staring at the front cover of a magazine with a photograph from the final of the French Open. The phone rang. It was my tennis club. What they wanted, I don't know. Something to do with my membership.

'I led a busy life, so I have very little time to notice these things. Lately I have had more time on my hands, and I have found myself noticing other 'little' incidents of this sort.

'Only a few months ago I had spent the day visiting all the places I went to routinely with my wife. Among all the memories, I had one constant and overriding thought. I kept telling myself, bleakly, that I must ensure my will stipulates that I am buried rather than cremated. 'Buried not cremated'; these were the words that went round my head on a loop. In the evening I went to a restaurant I have been to many times before. I am known there. I ate alone, but as I ate, I caught the conversation from the couple next to me. They were a young couple, and were having a playful discussion about whether it is better to be buried than cremated.

'Many examples of this sort of thing happened at work, but they do not stick out in my mind quite so much. These sort of 'coincidences' are easily explained in that context. It's not so strange that two or even three people should turn their attention to the same thing without declaring it. That's simply in the nature of the work. So even if these occurrences happened at work – and I am convinced they happened all the time – then they lend themselves too easily to reductive explanations.

'It's when this sort of thing happens in private, in moments of apparent intimacy, that I find it most interesting and memorable.

'Take, for example, a brief conversation I had only a few weeks ago with a close friend. I believe we had arranged to see each other for dinner. I said I would cook something here in my apartment. He came here. We chatted. I went to cook. As often happens when I cook, my mind wandered. I thought about a holiday Coumba and I took in the Ariége valley. We had walked one day fairly high up into the foothills of the Pyrénées. There we came across this wonderful old hamlet, now deserted. It had a well and a small lake, with enough faded memory to make the place ghostly. We walked by it, more or less in silence, taken in by its eerie serenity. We stopped by the well. I remember thinking idly – dreamily almost – that perhaps in the middle ages a cathar witch had been drowned in it. Coumba turned to me and said 'You enjoy silence too much.'

'And as I was recalling these events, my friend walked into the kitchen. He must have studied me for a moment, and then he said 'You take too much pleasure in silence.'"

Alice, whose curiosity was now tainted by alarm, said:

"You know, Rémy, there is a word for what you are describing."

But Rémy, for the moment, ignored the comment.

"I turned to look at my friend," he continued, "and I saw a look on his face. It was a look openly inviting me to make of his comment whatever I could. And then he hung his head and looked away."

Rémy paused very briefly.

"I remember that was the closest I ever came to a sensation that my own private reality was melting away before my eyes. It felt like my eyes were too weak to represent things around me in any stable form. I thought that even in this companion – a close, lifelong friend – there was no foundation."

"As I say ... " continued Alice before she was cut off.

"The word to which you were referring is 'paranoia'," said Rémy. "Am I right?"

"Yes," replied Alice.

"From what I have already said, you can begin to see that I have begun to understand paranoia. And the more you think paranoid thoughts, the more they box you in, but the more interesting and curious they become.

'I remember I once had a conversation with a stranger who was having some sort of breakdown. He told me that he had been having 'feelings of paranoia'. That was how he put it. I offered him some advice, and found out later that his paranoia was acute. He believed that people were coming to get him, and that they would take him away.

'When I looked back on it, the more I thought that his admission of paranoia was a way of testing the hardness of the world around him. 'I'm paranoid. That's crazy, right?' This was what he was saying, because he knew that as soon as someone he could vaguely trust said that he was being crazy, that gave him a stable vantage point from which to recover a sure perspective.

'But this person's paranoia ran deep. Again in retrospect I could see that, in spite of my reassurances, his mind was felling my words as I spoke them. 'These reassurances you are giving me, they – and you – are somehow part of the conspiracy. Don't ask me how I know it. I just do.' That's what he was thinking. Or something like it.

'If you ruminate too hard on this kind of thing, it rattles around your mind, and I believe it really can work you up into a state of delirium.

'I am a reflective sort of person, and I have thought about it. Like I say, I think I can begin to understand how a paranoid mind works. Those examples from my life that I have just given you; I have at times seen in them the evidence for some sort of conspiracy. Naturally, when you occupy a senior position in an office that carries with it a certain amount of power, this can turn a low-burning flame of suspicion into a roaring inferno. There is also something about the fast pace of ordinary working life that makes a habit out of this sort of suspicion.

'More recently, when I have found the time to relax and think more calmly, I have enjoyed imagining how a personal conspiracy might look.

'In the world of government, you can begin to imagine the kind of spooks who might be watching you, and you start to think wonderfully weird thoughts about everyone from the President of the Republic to your secretary. 'What do they know? Are they in on it? Is everyone in on it? Or is there a secret society at the heart of government, with extraordinary power at their means, to weave around me a web of baroque dreams?

'But surely, I then think to myself, this model of the world from which I am alienated, makes no sense. What about the phone call from my tennis club? What about the conversation in the restaurant about cremation versus burial? And what about my friend? Or should I say 'my friend'? Or the pair of you, for that matter? What should I make of you? And when you indulge those thoughts, you start to feel really crazy, and really lonely. I mean political conspiracies, even if they are far-fetched, at least have some historical precedent. But this more personal thinking becomes solipsistic in ways that only the most deranged mind can understand.

"Is there someone inside my mind,' you start to ask, 'anticipating my every move and reaction in synchrony with me? Are the people I interact with sustaining an illusion through which I cannot see but in which they are all somehow complicit? Is my every word, thought and most precious, private reaction broadcast to a secret audience?

'Disturbing as this way of thinking may at first seem, it actually makes the insipid side of routine life a little more interesting. I mean, if going to buy a carton of milk and some bread is not an act of mundane subsistence, but a piece of drama performed to a voyeuristic audience of millions, it at least makes everything a bit more thrilling! Or you can have fun with it in a different way. Suppose there are large numbers of people watching you in some prurient and intrusive way, waiting to catch a glimpse of your own intimate world, you can try your hardest to do absolutely nothing and be as dull as channel fog.

'If you push this way of thinking you can simultaneously doubt everything around you, while appearing to blithely go along with the illusion. Which brings me to you, and this conversation we are having right now.

'It's titillating to think that you, my wife, my wider family and friends are somehow unreal, or not what they appear to be. Occasionally I have sat down in a moment of relaxation and felt bewildered by how it might work. Your actions, responses and words would have to be coordinated and contrived, not only to 'appear' real to me, but to respond in some way to what I only think, rather than articulate. The sheer mechanics of the illusion confound my understanding, but then I suppose that's in the nature of a paranoid delusion. The 'real' world must in some way go beyond the only apparent world.

'And I have, once or twice, been sitting in front of someone, only to find myself thinking, as they speak; what's going on behind their face? Do they have some undetectable earpiece or some other communication device secreted about them? Or is their brain hardwired into the illusion, almost as though the person with whom I am speaking is only some sort of puppet or robot in a simulated universe, the delimitations of which I have long since forgotten? Unless, of course – and in some ways this would make more sense – I am the robot, and the scientific progeny of the world I inhabit?

'When I am thinking these things as someone is speaking to me, I also find myself thinking about what I am thinking, wondering if my thoughts have been planted or manipulated in some way to suit the conversation's overall theme and direction. Or, at other times, I will try to think things that might, covertly influence the nature of the conversation, or disorient and distract the coordinating powers that maintain my illusion.

'But, of course, if the conspiracy is as fundamental and programmatic as my 'delusion' construes it, then these thoughts are idle and futile (if they aren't anyway). If the conspiracy is real, then the illusion must be a condition for any thought I can possibly have. The conspiracy, in other words, presupposes that I inhabit something that is bigger, wider and deeper than the narrow dimensions of my own mind and body. So there is no thought that I could think which would interrupt the flow of a conversation. It is entirely determined. I am just a piece of code, programmed to behave in a particular way. And this means that even this conversation, the act of thinking and intriguing to speculatively unravel the conspiracy, must itself form part of its immanent determinations. Everything, guided by this way of thinking, is given. I suppose that is what makes it so frightening."

"Can't you hear yourself?" Alice interrupted suddenly. "This is crazy. I am telling you it's ... we are not part of any ... conspir ... this is crazy ... don't you realise that it's crazy? "

"Don't worry. Don't worry. I am only laying before you some of the things that have passed through my mind. I have not said – yet – that I give them any credence. They are just daydreams.

'And if you read a little about paranoia, you will understand that – apart from the profound disagreement it engenders among medical professionals – people are at their most susceptible to it when they are anxious. So there you are; I went through an anxious time, which means I am vulnerable to this particular bad habit of the mind. That's innocent enough, isn't it? In any case, there is a fault, I think, in these paranoid delusions, but it is the intuition from which the fault arises which interests me."

"What do you mean?"

"The fault is an inconsistency of reasoning. We are talking about extreme paranoia. Extreme paranoia. Pushed to its logical extreme this becomes solipsistic in the way I have already said. In other words you start to doubt even the most fundamental faculties of intuition: sight, touch, taste, sound, and of course the mind that gives them a diplomatic reception. But – and here is the contradiction – the mind is such a creature of habit that it can only use the faculties it doubts to imagine the nature of the conspiracy. Paranoia is, in other words, a sort of distorted and grotesque form of human nature. So we imagine a conspiracy of other human beings who, through advances in technology that to our comparatively mundane mind must seem fantastical, have access to our thoughts and the sensory signals with which we daily collide. And, with the advantage of this access, they can construct our reality or, in other words, 'pull the wool over our eyes'. This implies an order of reality that we can, however fancifully, use our faculties of sense and intelligence to imagine. But these are the very faculties we have just called into question! So we cannot construct this extreme paranoia coherently without contradicting it. It is logically impossible. If there is some elaborate and pervasive scheme from which the world around me is constructed, it hardly matters, because my ability to make sense of anything must itself be a condition of that scheme, which means I will only ever imagine the contorted angles of my own reflection. Paranoia is like being frightened by the sound of your own heartbeat!

'So, you will be pleased to know, that I do not think that you are part of a conspiracy against me. You may be less pleased to know that if there is a conspiracy it is probably also against you. But, as I say, that hardly matters.

'But the examples I have given from my own life – and I am sure there are examples you could adduce from other lives – to my way of thinking describe a human intuition; this is similar to a basic sense of danger, pain, pleasure, justice, love and so on. It is a sense of a complete picture from within an only partial view of the picture; it is a sense that a fuller, deeper view of things exists to which I don't have access. It is an intimation of perfection that intimates my own imperfection.

'It's quite common, I think, to find that paranoid minds believe that God or Jesus is talking to them. It might be a little unnerving for those who are in their 'right' mind, but perhaps paranoid minds really are in something like a direct conversation with God. Paranoia, I think, is a kind of surrender to the deafening noise of seraphic voices; which is why it must encounter human intelligence as a form of madness."

We didn't know what to make of this exactly. Rémy seemed to be admitting his paranoia while stripping away its layers of pathology. We kept quiet.

"I believe that, under the right circumstances, any mind is susceptible to the traits of paranoia," continued Rémy. "It is, so to speak, just a feature of human nature. Loneliness is one of the circumstances conducive to it. Looking back, if I think about the way I thought and sometimes behaved before I met my wife, I can see glimmers of these traits. But I am quite clear that keeping good company, or to have a companion, dampens their spirit. Having someone close to you whose company you respect, admire and enjoy ..." Rémy searched for his words, "... well, I found that my wife and I, between the two of us, created a kind of order, a world that was unique and new – quite new – for both of us. Some people talk about reality as though it is a brick wall erected to obstruct your path, something to which you must react passively. But, in my experience, if it is 'a wall', it is one that you build, almost always collaboratively, brick by brick. Which is why the kind of paranoia, scepticism, or solipsism I have been describing starts to take shape when there is no-one with whom to carry out the labour.

'So my chance encounter with a woman from a very different background to my own brought me into a kind of living I had not previously experienced. Between us, though it probably didn't always seem like it at the time, everything was good.

'If forbidding cracks threatened our happy little conjugal construction, then we just papered over them.

'But almost as soon as Coumba died – and compounded, of course, by the public embarrassment I was facing - this little world quickly came unstuck; and I became prey to all the strange solitary thoughts I have mentioned. Not that I want to give the impression that at one moment the world seemed bright and full of meaning, and all of a sudden it turned dark. It did not work like that. My marriage gave me a quiet confidence, and at the time I thought it gave me a clear-sighted view of things. In fact it did give me a clear view of things, in the sense that I can still remember how clearly I saw everything; but when it came to its abrupt end, all the things I had seen clearly started to seem more fragile, or less confident and clear. Not that it destroyed everything that was good in our relationship, except in the most obvious sense. Instead it made me look at it through a different lens. It circumscribed and enshrined it, like the architectural biography of a tomb. It feels to me like I was glimpsing how the shape and characteristics of a life must look from beyond the grave; as though straying close to the edges that make something finite.

'People talk about 'falling in love'. It's a very suitable image. I didn't feel in control when I fell in love. I think that's why I kept it a secret; because I couldn't make any sense of it. You fall into it, and it sort of carries you along. It picks you up and away you go. I didn't really know or understand anything about it, except that, in a clumsy sort of way, I thought it was important to me, and that it absolved me from the odd, introverted existence I had led until then.

'But the ability to look back on something – to reflect – I don't think should be ignored. And the more I reflect, the more I think my marriage was something that suited me; it was right for me; it made sense (even if nothing at the time made sense). To analyse it coldly at a distance – a practice in which I have some experience – it seems well-contrived, even perhaps to suggest an order, a structure or purpose. This means that, separated only by time and judgement, a single experience can be chaotic and determined, irrational and rational. This recollection of something ordered smuggled into disorder ... well, it interests me.

'I find it interesting because, in different ways, my experience of both has been tidal; at one time withdrawing into empty introspection, and at another returning to a life of sorts. This is not so unusual. People have their good days and bad days, after all. That's nothing new. But I see in some other people, even in the face of the adversity I have described, a more or less constant will to make something out of the world around them. They fight against the tide. It is as though there is only one state in which life rightfully belongs and to achieve it requires unrelenting commitment and resolve. I, on the other hand, seem to rise and fall with the tide. But that image doesn't quite work, does it? It just suggests moving between two different states without allowing that the nature of those states might influence each other."

"What do you mean?" asked Alice.

"I don't know – imagine you are a schoolboy in a line of other schoolboys waiting to be selected by the team captains of two football teams. You are the last person they select. This upsets you so, after that, you work on your game – maybe you practice at home or something. Word gets around and the team captains realise that you are more of an asset than they thought you were, so next time you are waiting to be selected they pick you ahead of others. And in that way you are reintroduced to that particular community of 90 minutes. But have you simply achieved what you originally hoped to achieve? I'm not so sure. In my case anyway, like it or not, the original rejection has changed you in some way. At the very least you do not walk into the game with the unquestioning self-confidence of the boys with twinkle toes! I even think that if you find yourself called repeatedly to a game you aren't very well suited to play – so that you know it and those calling you know it – you must eventually see the game in a very different way. You might even resent it and want to reject it, don't you think? Even if you don't go quite that far, a measure of weariness might surface that puts some distance between your true centre of gravity and the other players; you might look at it all more philosophically.

'This is what I mean when I talk about reflection. To be, albeit temporarily, cut off from things and then to return to them gives an insight into how they look from the outside; and in seeing everything in a different way it changes how you behave towards them.

'I am sorry to talk about this at such length; but if it surprises you that I can talk so much about something so apparently dismal, then you are wrong. The reason I can talk so effusively about it is for the reason I have just given: that the changed perspective is strangely invigorating, memorable or stimulating, much more so, I imagine, than any short-term personal triumph. This is the odd thing, the paradoxical thing, about everything that happened to me back in the 1990s: the bombardment of 'bad luck' I experienced did leave me feeling wounded, battered and assaulted. But it was only 'bad' from the perspective of the narrow self-interests I may have had at the time.

'This was one of the most peculiar and frightening things about everything that happened to me. Though by its own logic, it begins to reach a point where the meaning of words like 'frightening' are unclear. The kind of conspiracy-theorist mind I was talking about earlier follows the same line of thought. In that case, you would think that, by definition, any person in their 'right frame of mind' – though again, what does that mean eh? – would naturally recognise that level of paranoia as a form of mental illness and look for a cure: meaning the return to a 'right frame of mind'. I suppose that's all very sensible and the experiences of many people would reckon that perspective natural. So, I expect it is natural. But, if there are other people like me (granted I might be a little eccentric!), then they too will move with the tides. By that I mean, even if they are 'brought back' to a right frame of mind, they are not entirely restored to what they were previously. Their 'illness' has changed them; a trace of it remains about them, sort of like a scar or a limp. But the 'frightening' thought is that this is not quite as frightening as it might seem. The loss of all perspective in something like a paranoid mind, in so far as you are aware of it at all, grabs you by the very seat of your existence and seems to pull, so that everything suddenly becomes more intense, even more real and alive, like you are witnessing death and birth simultaneously.

'That's why I say that acts of reflection – acts of reflection like this – are important, because written all over them is the recollection of that intensity. They don't destroy past relationships (or current relationships like yours); they build them up into something with more dimension and structure.

'And it seems to me that it is this dimension and structure that the memory we are all sharing has provided. I have already said, I think that the story of The Artisan's Wife and its different uses is designed to recall something, but that the ultimate object of memory is not something to which I, or anyone, have a unique claim. This tells me that my marriage was itself the reflection of something beyond itself, and that's how it could discover any sustained meaning at all. Love, they say, is not rude."

"What is the memory, then?" asked Alice daring to indulge the broad thrust of Rémy's thought.

"I am not sure exactly, but it seems to be talking back to us, wouldn't you say?"

"Talking back to us?"

"Or even having fun with us."

"Fun?"

"Wouldn't you say?"

"I'm not sure I ... it's all ... there's a lot to take on board ... " She sounded doubtful.

"What's it saying?" I asked.

"It's telling you something you already know but – quite obviously – have forgotten. Not only that, but it's telling you something that you want to remember. I don't imagine for a minute that you feel indifferent about all this."

"Damn right," said Alice.

"Where does it come from? This memory – how did we find it? Did we discover it or did it discover us? And if so, when and how? What part of our minds did it infiltrate? At what point, and how did it pass so unnoticed, so undecided and unchosen? Is it, like all memories, something waiting in the deepest, darkest interstices of the mind for the right circumstances to invite it out of the shadows?"

"I don't know," said Alice.

"Nor do I," I said.

"Exactly," replied Rémy running wild, "this is not an impression on a wax tablet; it's not a photograph rendered in faded form on the back of our skulls that we can only dimly recall. This is not a memory that fills your nostrils, that you have pawed softly, that has tingled on your tongue or pounded at your ears."

It seemed too obvious to ask "Well where has it come from, then?" and I was convinced that Rémy was about to tell us anyway, so I kept quiet. All the same, my mind mused over the possibilities. Were we talking about some sort of special computer chip? Were the three of us unsuspecting participants in a cutting-edge experiment in psychological warfare sponsored by western governments? Had we all been programmed with this script to explore how far states could manipulate the minds of their enemies? I thought this was pretty unlikely. Why would they choose an obscure Russian film? That there was a senior intelligence officer in the pentagon who had a secret penchant for early twentieth century pre-soviet silent film was about as improbable as it could get.

Alice's face was fairly transparent to the view that all of this did not really add up to an 'explanation' but was closer to the midnight meanderings of an untied mind.

"So, you're saying it didn't happen? That's what you're saying? If it didn't happen in any of those ways, then it didn't happen at all. Surely. That's only logical."

"But it did happen. We know it happened. It happened yesterday and on Friday."

"After we knew it had already happened."

"That's just it. That's the point. The memory comes before the sensory form it takes. It is not derived through the senses, but for them."

"That doesn't make any sense."

"Well ... I suppose ..."

"You agree?"

"Did we ever disagree? We both agree that something happened, the order in which it happened and that this is, in some ways, nonsense."

Rémy gave a sort of truncated chuckle.

Alice looked like she was clamping the subject matter between the two sides of her brain.

"What do you understand by the word 'nonsense'?"

"There are different perspectives."

As Rémy began a furtive defense of nonsense, I knew I was swayed, but held in check by an inner voice of reason telling me not to be so silly and to keep my feet firmly on the ground. But in the slapstick split-personality disorder the discussion was beginning to engender in me, I was happy to start dallying with the notion that 'nonsense' might be a credible state from which to proceed through life. Was I about to don a child's potty for a hat and read poetry to the furniture?

"And how could we have ever known this story of the film, much less recite it word for word (if we have been reciting it word for word – you see I don't even know that)?"

"You have been reciting it word for word. You do know that. Of course you know it."

"This is crazy."

"Well … I won't argue with you. And yet the memory also makes a curious kind of sense out of things."

"So sense is nonsense and vice versa?"

"There are different perspectives."

"Yes, the perspective of sense and the perspective of nonsense. Which side are you on?"

"I prefer not to think about it quite so categorically."

"What?!"

"And we agree. Generally speaking, I think we agree, don't we?"

"Do we?"

"If you step back and analyse it."

"We seem to be bashing our 'agreement' back and forth quite a lot."

"But do you disagree with what I have said?"

"What you have said makes no sense."

Rémy dwelled on this comment for a moment.

"Are you sure about that? You see, it seems to me that we are living witnesses to its sense. I said a moment ago that the memory is talking back to us; as though it has found a temporary purpose. More particularly … here's what I think … you will not give it much time, I am sure … but I think the memory is talking back to you. The two of you. Somehow or another, you need it. It has shaped itself around your lives. Why exactly, I don't know. Perhaps only you know that. But it seems clear to me that, if that is the case, then it has fashioned a presence among us for a reason.

'So, as I have said, we are living witnesses to its sense. If anything is crazy, the memory seems to be telling us that, after a fashion, we are. 'Sense', if it ever really exists, only emerges, through us, from somewhere else."

By this stage I was not at all confident about the general state of my mental health and was feeling nostalgic for the honey and cheese.

HANDS AND BODIES

My Dear Coumba,

Today I went into the city. I walked around for a while, visiting some of my old haunts. I do not do this very often. Nowadays I only travel to the city when it is absolutely necessary. I prefer privacy.

But, for some reason I cannot explain, I have found myself thinking lately about my old working routines: the cafés and bars I visited, the restaurants at which I ate with colleagues and dignitaries. So I decided to return to them on my own, as a man of leisure.

I drove into the city and I spent some time walking, sitting, looking at things, as a ghost looking outside-in on his life. It was a peculiar experience. When I looked around at everyone else they were all so immersed in the activities, routines, compulsions of their life; whereas I was merely an observer.

This made me realise that I had been pushed out of, not

only my work, but also all the soft social experiences that go with it.

As I sat there thinking about this (and after a glass of wine) I felt a sudden headstrong rush of will to fight against the thrust of human behaviour that had confined me to this strange spectre of the past, invisible to everyone. I felt a sudden urge to yank on the sleeves of strangers, or tap them on the shoulder and say “Look, here I am – do you see me? I am here talking to you, you know. Well, what have you got to say about that?!”

An instinct is, of course, one thing, and, as you know, I have never been quite so impulsive. So I acted on my impulse with a little more prudence and finesse. I walked up to the bar. I ordered another glass of wine. I talked to the barman. Some of the other barflies joined in our conversation and banter. And it turned into a very enjoyable afternoon. We joked about things: how the city has changed, our love lives, even taxation.

You would, no doubt, not approve, Coumba, but I must confess that I became quite drunk, and in no time at all, turned into one of those house drunkards that regular clientele try their hardest to avoid.

I also found that these men who drink together around the bar are a magnet for weirdos.

In the early evening a young man came into the bar and took a seat next to me. We began talking, and I quickly found out that he was a student. This was not peculiar, because he could easily have been a student. But there was something about his manner that suggested he was not, despite his innocent claim, telling the truth. We talked some more: "So what are you studying?" I asked.

"Hands," he said.

"Hands?" I said. "You mean ... ?" and I held up both my hands.

"Yes, that's right. Hands," he replied shortly, in a way that hinted I was being unusually stupid.

"So, some sort of medicine?" I asked.

"Medicine?!" he exclaimed, becoming even more incredulous. "Why do you say that?"

"I just thought that it must be ..."

I was eager to defend the intuitive and rational centre of my question.

"I don't study medicine," he said. "Just hands."

In his mind this seemed to clear up the matter.

"Forgive me," I continued, "as you can see, I have had one or two glasses of wine. If it isn't within the broader field of medicine, what can it be? Perhaps some sort of robotics?"

"No, no," his frown cutting deeper still, "I am not studying robotics or medicine. I am studying hands."

I persevered.

"I understand that you are studying hands, but as far as I am aware 'the study of hands' is not a discipline that any university recognises, except perhaps as a specialism within another subject. Hence I was guessing at medicine or robotics."

The young man would not be swayed by my line of thought.

"I am studying hands and that's all."

"Well, that's good," I said eventually. "It's good to have a subject. It's good to have something to study."

The young man, I sensed, wasn't really listening. Instead, he repeated 'just hands' firmly and with a sort of defensive conviction.

I should have let it go, but a part of me wanted to keep probing.

"If you don't mind my asking," I went on, after I had taken a few more mouthfuls of wine, "what, specifically, do you study when you study hands?"

This question changed the young man's entire demeanour. His face lit up. But he did not say anything. He rolled up one of his sleeves to the elbow, raised his arm and then lowered it to the bar. He arched his hand, in the way that a spider arches its back, and tapped the bar with each of his fingers.

He turned to look at me.

"Do you see?" he asked, still excited.

"I honestly wanted to say 'yes'."

"No," I said. "The tapping?"

The young man raised his arm again and held the back of his hand to my face.

"The movement. The hand and its movement. This is a form of art. Of delicate taste and refinement that must be studied carefully and cultivated."

He spoke these words slowly, choosing each one carefully.

"I see," I said.

The young man's brains were barbecued.

"Yes, now that you mention it, I see. There is a good deal

of artistry in the way hands move."

"And sometimes," interrupted the young man, "even when they don't."

"Of course, of course. Things can be quite beautiful when they are still."

I tapped my fingers on the bar.

"Tap, tap, tap," I said, looking at my hand, "yes, quite beautiful."

"Oh, but not like that," said the young man. "No your hands are not beautiful when you do it like that."

"No?" I said.

"All hands are beautiful, but we have to treat them in the right way. That's why it is important to study them. Watch me. Like this."

Once again he arched his hand over the bar, and tapped it with his fingers, one-by-one. I tried to imitate the young man.

"Like this?" I asked.

"Nearly," he replied, and reaching across, inserted his index finger under the palm of my hand and gave it a few sharp pokes to raise the arch in my hand and wrist. I felt sure that we must have looked like a pair of human mosquitoes reaching out to the bar with effete proboscises.

Others had overheard our conversation, including the barman.

"What about feet?" asked the barman. "Do you study feet?"

"Interesting thought," I nodded. "Yes, what about feet?"

"No, I don't study feet," said the young man. "But I can see how they might be interesting."

"Hands are your real passion?" I asked, sharing a wink with the barman.

"There is so much to study."

"You mean, their movements?"

"Yes, in their movements. There is so much to study."

"What about knees?" said someone sitting nearby.

The young man shrugged his shoulder with a look of innocent exhaustion.

"Again, I can see that knees have many interesting characteristics."

"You mean ... hair?" asked the barman.

"But," continued the young man, "I am many, many years away from completing my research into hands."

"Years?" asked the barman, who was now looking amused.

"My analysis takes time. It requires close observation and precision."

"Yes, I see," I said.

"Arse!" said someone loudly.

We all drank.

"Yes, so it's all in the hands," I said. "A fascinating area of study."

"But what about your head? Surely a head must be interesting?" asked the barman earnestly.

"No," said the young man, "I am less interested in the head."

He looked distastefully at the barman. The barman was genuinely confused.

"But I don't understand," he replied. "How can you not be interested in the head?" he asked.

"The head doesn't interest me," said the young man, terse and dismissive.

"But," the barman came back, reasoning his way, "to study hands you must have to use your head. So you need your head in order to have any interest at all in hands."

"I don't accept that line of reasoning," said the young man.

Those of us around collectively exhaled a short laugh.

"What do you mean?" I asked.

"Just as I say: I don't accept the logic."

"But you can't even look at a hand without using your head."

"I very much deny that."

"Arse!" shouted the same voice.

"But you can't eyeball a hand with a fingernail or a cuticle."

Another stranger quickly cut in.

"Some of us do think with our ... "

" ... shut it!" said the barman, cutting him off.

The young man stood as if to leave.

"I must excuse myself gentlemen. I am prepared to accept that there are many other interesting areas of study, but the nature of the task and the limited time and resource available to me, mean that I must, perforce, constrain my study to my first love and interest: the study of hands."

And with these remarks he walked out of the bar.

So here you have in writing, my dear Coumba, a full and frank account of my encounter with a young student fixated on the study of hands to the exclusion of the anatomic whole.

All my love
Rémy

LA GOLONDRINA

Alice wanted to talk. In the car, her mind was almost as noisy as the engine. And she wanted to give her thoughts immediate satisfaction, which produced faltering, unfinished remarks and half-formulated questions. Her impatience was hard at work.

The events of the morning kept dragging her back, halting her attempts to make sense of it. 'What did he mean when he said ...?' and 'But that didn't fit with that thing he said about ...' - these were the sort of incomplete musings which blocked the way to lucid interpretation.

"What did you make of it?" she would begin, but then interrupt me before I could attempt an answer.

Which was fine by me because I didn't want to attempt an answer. I had no idea what to make of it. It didn't really make any sense.

Her jitteriness made me nervous, and I felt uncomfortable sitting next to her, as I waited for a question, a frustration, even the withheld prospect of physical violence. It didn't seem impossible that she might, irrationally, lash out over the gearbox to punch me in the ribs with her right hand. In the odd moments I managed to relax, my mind turned towards the zoetrope of Parisian scenery as it flashed by. I wanted to daydream.

We were trying to remember something we had never experienced; and the memory was trying to tell us something. My questions were 'What?' and then 'What?' again. Alice, unlike me, was capable of arranging her thoughts and then articulating them clearly. But, in my case, my 'analysis' would only emerge as a failed attempt to make polite conversation – it would default to a sort of stoical, British politeness. It was a struggle, but I managed to suppress the urge to say 'Well, interesting morning'. I somehow thought that Alice might slap me in the face again if I said that.

It all seemed a bit like trying to do advanced algebra in my head, and, after a moment of studious concentration, I was prepared to chuck my brain out of the window. And yet, when I did this, another question kept coming back to me: 'Why had I come to Paris?'

I knew the answer. Or partly knew it. I had tried, in my own way, to explain it to Alice when we had eaten out together the day before. She hadn't been satisfied. Not by a long way. And, truthfully, I wasn't satisfied either. I had surfaced part of the answer, but not really drilled down to the dark, dead heart of the matter.

Why had I come to Paris? The city of lights. The city of lovers and artists.

As the car pulled up to the curb, the answer was obvious:

Because I had never been in love, and I wanted to be.

The dog barked at us, as we alighted from the car. I looked round. Alice tried to peer over the chassis.

"What's that?" she said.

It was the dog. Our dog. The same creature we had chased around the streets on Friday. The same canine I had spotted – twice – the day before. It was loitering by the rear wheel of the car, staring up at me, with accusatory eyes.

"The dog!" said Alice, when she had run around to the passenger side.

The dog barked.

This was too much for her. She had no idea how to make sense of it.

"Well that's ..." she began.

The dog barked again. Then he raised his back leg and urinated on her rear wheel.

"You know, I'm fairly sure this dog is trying to tell us something," I said.

"He just pissed on my car."

"Even so."

"I can't cope with this," said Alice. "I think I might be having a nervous breakdown."

I kneeled down to the dog's level. He lowered his head, and backed off nervously.

"What is it? What are you trying to tell us?"

I held out my hand. The dog licked it. Then he turned a complete circle, and arched the front half of his body, as if to turn again.

"He wants us ..."

"... No!" said Alice peremptorily. "I'm sorry I've had enough of it. I'm going home. I'm going to bed. I need to think about it. Or get drunk. Probably get drunk."

"Aren't you curious?" I said.

"No."

The dog let out a short high-pitched crying noise.

"I think he's upset," I said.

"The little poppet," said Alice sarcastically.

But the dog was having none of it. He shot through my legs, and jumped up at Alice. In a single leap, he grabbed her handbag in his mouth, pulling it to the ground. Its contents scattered all over the floor, and the dog immediately seized her purse between his jaws, then hightailed off down the street.

I looked at Alice in disbelief, as she picked up her presence of mind from the mess on the floor. Our dog was no friend. He was a trained thief!

"Don't just stand there," she said. "Get after him!"

"Oh ... yes!" I stammered.

I ran down the street after the dog.

I thought, at first, that I stood no chance. Even with no head start, the dog would outrun me. And if he was a street-savvy canine, he would know his way down every side-street and alleyway, into the terrible troglodyte world beneath the semblance of law and order.

So I was surprised to see him weaving between some bollards and the cobblestones. He saw me straight away. He even dropped the loot to get a good look. I didn't run. I walked towards him calmly. The dog appeared to consider me as I approached, but it was difficult to get the measure of his mind. What was he thinking? Was he thinking?

Just as I was getting close, he picked up the purse again, and scampered off.

“Wait!” I called after him.

My feet were killing me, but I managed to keep going.

The dog took me all the way down another street. I had to dodge a mixture of trees, bollards and people to keep up with him. Then he darted down a back alley at full pace. I just caught his tail disappearing from sight. When I turned the corner, and looked down the alley, I could see nothing: no trees, no bollards, no people. And no dog. I kept up the pursuit all the same, and at the same speed, though my chest was starting to complain. I must have run a full three quarters of the way down the alley when, before I knew it, I was flying, then falling, then hurting. I was aware of pain in my right knee, my right hip, my right elbow and the palms of both hands.

I heard a voice near me. A shadow appeared in my peripheral vision, which knelt down at my side, exclaiming shock, sympathy and testing my stunned state of mind with unintelligible questions.

The man grabbed me by the elbow. He was clean-shaven, with neat close-cropped black hair, chestnut eyes and a geometric jaw. He wore a simple white shirt, blue jeans, and blue suede ankle boots.

I found it hard to speak at first, but finally I managed to spit out a few blood-stained fragments of sense.

“I ... I’m ... no, I’m fine ... I’m English ... I don’t ... er ... I don't ..."

"English? You are English. I er ... J'ai ... mais non ... okay? You are hurt, non?"

"No, I'm ... I'm not ... just a little scratched ... but I'm ... thank you ... I'm ..."

I stopped trying to speak. The dog walked up to me. It was still carrying the purse in its mouth. It lowered its head, and dropped it on the ground. Its eyes looked at me, down at the purse, then back to me. It looked like it wanted me to play fetch.

The dog was panting. I was panting.

"You are sure?" said the man.

The dog nudged the purse with his nose.

I exhaled loudly.

"Bad dog!" said the man, and followed it through with a stern reprimand in French. "He jump out from the ... the ... and ... you see ... he get between your legs, so that you ...You must have ... what have you ... ç'est quoi ça?"

The man started to think about the scene before him. He picked up the purse.

"This ... it's yours?" he said, waving the purse in my face.

"Not mine. A friend of mine's."

Slowly, thoughtfully, the man handed me the purse, and helped me to my feet.

"You know this dog?" he asked.

"That might be going a bit far. Our paths have crossed."

"He doesn't belong to you?"

"No."

"But he steal your ... your friend's ... wallet?"

"So it seems."

"I must ask – how you have ... how have you met these dogs ... this dog before now?"

I shrugged my shoulders.

"He started to follow me (and my friend) a couple of days ago. We shooed him away. I saw him again yesterday. Then today, he appeared again. He jumped up at my friend, knocked her handbag from her hands, and ... he ... well, he took her purse."

"Ha ha! Daylight robbery!"

The man studied the dog, who still had his eyes fixed stubbornly on me.

"He is a strange one," said the man.

"Yes," I said, then something occurred to me. "Do you know him too?"

"I mean, like you, it is a bit far to say this, but this dog, he has stayed with me for a few day. He has come on 'oliday to my 'ouse."

"Since when?" I asked.

"Ah ... He does not belong to you?"

"No."

"Your name is not ... What is your name?"

"Sam," I said.

"Ah. Not Lanier?"

"No."

"Ah."

I thought about it.

"What did you say?"

"Pardon?"

"What … you asked me a question. Just then."

"You are not Lanier?"

"Why? … I'm not called Lanier. But why do you ask?"

"Because he belong to Lanier. On his … on … er … around his …"

The man gestured around his neck.

"His collar?"

"Yes. This is the word, I think. It say, he belong to … he belong to Lanier."

"Lanier? You're sure."

"Yes, of course. Please."

The man bent down, took the dog by its collar and showed me the tag. It read:

Lanier
56 Rue d'Amsterdam

"Lanier," I said in disbelief.

"You are not Lanier?"

"No."

"But you know Lanier?"

I thought.

"No," I said.

"No?"

"No."

"You don't know him? But the name … you know the name?"

"Sort of."

Then something even more peculiar happened. I heard

a loud bang. Or thought I did. The sound erupted from nowhere, or if I were to guess where it might have come from, I would say it began somewhere in the elusive pulses of my mind. I must have looked like I had been punched in the face. The noise was so loud, it made me stagger backwards and reach out for something to hold onto.

"Are you all right?" the man asked.

Had he not heard the noise?

"Yes," I said, quick to my composure, and searching his face for signs of shock, or at least some kind of reaction.

He hadn't heard it. What was going on?

"You ... you look ... you are sure?" said the man.

"I just heard ... but you didn't ... ?"

The man shook his head.

"I expect I'm just a little rattled."

Even the dog looked up at me with concern.

"It's just a name – Lanier, I mean – that I came across in the last few days. But it's nothing, really. Just a coincidence."

"Perhaps it must be; but you know something, I have been to this place – there is no Lanier at 56 Rue d'Amsterdam. I check."

"Yes?"

"It's strange."

"Yes."

The man switched tack.

"I'm sorry, we are standing on the street, and you are ... would you like to come inside. You can sit down. Er ... drink?"

"Oh, no, thank you. That's kind. But I should really get back to my ... she just wants her purse. I'm sure she must be wondering where I am."

"You are sure ... perhaps you have ... ah ..."

The man wriggled his fingers before his forehead.

"Concussion?"

"Yes."

"It's all right. Honestly. I didn't bang my head. I am a little shaken, that's all. But I'm fine. And I should be getting back. I have the purse, after all. Thank you for your concern. It was very kind."

The man shrugged his shoulders.

I turned to walk back down the alley with a slight limp, clutching the purse. I had gone a little way when I heard a whistle. I turned around. The man stood in the same spot, watching the dog as it trundled after me.

The man opened his arms and shrugged his shoulders again, as if to say 'What can I do?'

And he was right. What could he do? Or what could I do? Neither of us had custody over the dog. So it was free to do as it pleased. If it wanted to follow me, I couldn't stop it. Neither of us, after all, was Lanier.

Alice's home was not what I expected. I thought it would exude her character. I thought her tastes and opinions would have, consciously or unconsciously, shown up in the décor, the choice of furnishings, the tonal subtleties of the wallpaper. But everything about the apartment was strangely empty. I could almost walk into one of the rooms, and point at all the spaces where it looked like something was missing. And this was not a composition artfully reduced to a minimalist repetition of simple musical patterns; it was simple, unreflective silence.

I examined each room, as Alice milled about offering me bowls of olives and glasses of mint cordial. Was it, I thought, that her body absorbed so much of her personality that she had little to spare? Or was her outward personality something much more brittle than it at first seemed? One way or the other, I found that these gaps in the decorating only made Alice a more interesting person.

I also had the feeling that, at home, she was less 'at home' around me. Her short-sighted sense of hospitality dazzled her into murmured apologies, and hints of girlish embarrassment.

"I've plenty of toilet paper, you know," she said, only half-joking and apparently on the assumption that this was a necessary reassurance.

I settled into one of her armchairs. She settled on the sofa opposite, a pair of varifocal glasses perched on the end of her nose. Over her shoulder, I could see a framed photograph of a blonde-haired girl in a scarf, her cheeks in full flush. She was standing somewhere in London that looked a little like Bloomsbury.

"That's my daughter," said Alice.

"I thought it might be."

The dog had trailed me around the flat like a page girl. Then it slumped on the floor to my right, lying on its stomach at full spread. It panted a little, was startled by odd noises and the strangely vacant room, and then rested its head on its paws. Alice hadn't been pleased about admitting it. But so many inexplicable surprises had kicked her in the teeth that she acquiesced to its presence in her home without putting up too much of a fight. I promised her that I would explain.

Something about Alice had changed. I had noticed it as we were driving back from Rémy's. It showed in her silence. This was not too surprising. We had plenty to think about, after all. But my previous experience of Alice had been that she did most of her thinking out loud, and that introspection was at best a tolerable eccentricity in other people.

She didn't even give me a clue. Rémy had covered so much ground it was impossible to know what specifically sailed over the surface of her mind. Or was she thinking about it at all? Perhaps that was the answer; perhaps there was so much to weigh up that it was too much.

"Are you sure you wouldn't like anything to drink?" she asked mechanically and with no apparent thought.

"Tea perhaps. Do you have tea?" I asked.

"I have tea," she replied.

She went off towards the kitchen.

"Make yourself at home," she said. "I won't be a minute."

I leaned back in my chair, revisiting, in a bovine and generally slow-to-move-forward way, my curiosity about the apartment's absence of character. I spent a few moments thinking about the lack of anything to think about. I sensed the dog was doing the same.

Once I had exhausted my interest in Alice's voided apartment, I needed something else to distract me. At first I thought about the dog, and about Lanier, the character I was 'playing' in the film. How was it possible that the dog could be owned by a fictitious character? It really didn't make sense, so I tried to think about something else. Which led me back to the morning.

As we were leaving Rémy's apartment and making arrangements for the final rendez vous later in the day, he had kissed Alice on the cheeks and shook me by the hand. Then he had said:

"I'm sure you must be leaving me with one overriding thought: this man requires medical help. This man is unwell."

He didn't say these words solemnly or sadly, but suggestively as though he wanted to plant this impression in our minds and encourage us to question it. Whatever else Alice had been thinking about, I was sure that this last statement figured. I know that it figured for me. But, perhaps unlike Alice, once I had turned it over in my mind a few times, I let it go. The rhythm of the car and witnessing the streets of Paris had taken over.

"I'll let it brew," said Alice, returning to the room.

"Thanks."

"So how are we?"

"Yes," I hesitated, "all right."

She glanced at the dog.

"Busy day," she said.

"Yes."

Then she snorted.

She looked at me curiously; and then, felled by a thought, she pulled up a chair from the nearby table and sat down.

"So first things first; let's talk about Rémy. We can do the dog afterwards. What do you think?"

"All right."

"So … dare I ask? … What did you make of it all?" she asked eventually.

I thought for a while.

"I don't know exactly," I replied. "I'm not sure what to make of it exactly."

"Do you think he was …?" she stopped in this act of wondering out loud, so that I could only guess at the final words of her question. "There was, I am sure, some kind of trickery at work. He had a glimmer in his eye."

She didn't hold onto this thought.

"Do you know what I made of it?" she asked.

"What?"

"I'm sure I'll keep thinking about it … but it makes me feel … I feel ridiculous telling you this … do you remember, a couple of days ago when we first met, I told you that I have always felt angry that the world around me would not … it had no place for the romantic naivety of a young girl … it bullies you into a notion of the 'real' world. But as I sat there listening to him …being … I was cynical … the shadow of the past managed to creep up on me. It was strange. And of all the things I should be thinking about, this is the one thing that bothers me most."

"That is?"

"Yes."

"Why?"

A ripple across the surface of her face suggested that

Alice had experienced a groundswell of feeling that was too sudden and immense to articulate. Her right arm cast around over the surface of the dining table. Her fingers grazed against a bowl of olives; and, apparently unable to vent the contents of her mind and body in any other way, she picked an olive out of the bowl and threw it at me, so that it hit me on the side of the head and bounced onto the floor. I looked at the coffee table in shock and, in the absence of anything rational, for a causal explanation. My eyes turned back to Alice.

"I'm sorry," she said. "I didn't mean to throw an appetiser at your head."

"Is the answer that obvious?" I asked.

"No, it isn't obvious at all," she said irritably. "That's why I ..."

She stood up.

"Oh, I see."

She paced.

Would she pick up the olive, I wondered.

"There was a glimmer in his eye. Don't you think? Didn't you notice it?"

"Perhaps," I replied, "why, you think he wasn't telling the truth?"

She gave a short laugh.

I could almost see Alice's mind turning it over and the product of her thoughts appearing in a neat little production-line for my inspection and approval.

"That last thing he said. He was trying – trying, you see – to make us understand that he could almost see things from our point of view. All the detail he gave us. It was too … it was something he had planned and premeditated."

"So? I thought that was part of the point."

"Perhaps, but there was an almost lawyerly consideration for detail. And that last point – what he said about needing medical help – it was like he was showing us that he was cool-headed. He wanted to set everything out at a distance, and say: 'So, what do you make of that, then?' It was a sort of trick or taunt. As if he were saying 'Many of the things I have described about my state of mind show that I am mentally unwell. But I can see all this with the clarity of a medical mind. So what do you think? Am I unwell?'"

Alice was right that this appeared to be the meaning of his final statement, but she was hinting at its meaning and significance in a way that I could not grasp.

"What do you take away from that?" I asked.

I could see, immediately, that she didn't know exactly but was working it all out as she spoke.

"Well I can't speak for you obviously," she began – a point which seemed so banal it was not worth mentioning, but which made me worry that she had been thinking things that I hadn't – "but that statement he left us with stood at the end of a line of thoughts that I have kept to myself over the last couple of days."

I found it hard to believe that Alice kept anything to herself, but I was prepared to indulge her.

"What do you mean?" I asked, my eyes searching the floor for the olive she had thrown at me.

"After the first scene – you know, the one outside the

church – my first thought (after I had overcome the shock) was that this was a trick and that we were being deceived. I suppose my suspicion fell on Rémy first of all.

'Then, after the second scene, I thought it might be you. You were – you are – too passive and accepting (it bothers me even now). That wasn't right, I thought. I thought it was ... reluctant as I might be to admit it ... I thought it was a conspiracy against me. That's my point. I had stumbled into exactly the same frame of mind that Rémy was describing to us earlier. Those last words of his were deliberate. He wasn't just saying 'What do you make of that, then?' He was saying 'You know exactly what to make of that because you're thinking in the same way. You're sharing my madness.'"

Alice was now looking a little wound up by where her own trail of reasoning had led her.

"Do you remember the story of the film?" she continued.

"The Artisan's ...?"

"...Yes. In both the story of the film and the story of the actress who was in it, she finds what she is looking for when the problem of her identity is resolved; when her paramour finds out who she really is. Or when she decides who she really is. It often works like that, doesn't it?"

She was starting to sound a little melancholy.

"If I try to make sense of our amnesia from my point of view I just become the kind of fruitcake that Rémy described. Who are you? You are ... well, who knows? It could be someone conspiring against me in any number of ways: a student prank, the trick of an ex-husband. You name it. Whatever the case, I don't know who you are – and let's face it, I don't know who you are. And I don't know who Rémy is, just like you don't know. And you don't know who I am. Nobody really knows anything if you think about this memory just from your own perspective. You and I – we're just unconnected words that, in isolation, don't mean anything. We are ridiculous. And even if we were to collide, what would that mean?

'When you begin to look at it like that ... I mean, you can see how doubting really would drive you insane. The paranoia ... Which means that it's very simple: the only move left is to ... to accept the memory."

Alice picked up another olive. She looked at it.

"When I was younger, I just wanted to scream and shout, and knock things down. Not for its own sake; not in a gratuitous way. But because of all the weird, deferential, bottom-patting set of rules that choked the life blood ... God I wanted to scream. You have no idea ... how many times ... and even now ... I don't know ..."

She threw the olive at my head again. It bounced off the top of my forehead, onto the arm of the armchair and then the floor. I tried not to blink.

"I'm sorry. It all makes me ... I shouldn't reflect on my own ... I suppose that's the point. But do you see? Do you see what I was trying to say to you the other day?"

I shook my head in a way that made me look like I wanted to say 'Yes'.

"Argh ... damn it."

She picked up another olive in her frustration. My body tensed.

"Sorry," I said.

She looked me over out of curiosity.

"What I've been saying – does it make sense?"

She sounded nervous and I must have looked frightened.

"I ..." I began, but didn't know what I wanted to say, except that I wanted to say something that might turn around Alice's condemnation.

"It makes me feel a little sad. That's all I'm saying," she said. "You like to think that you have the freedom to make the right choices for yourself. But even I can see that ... there was a mould and I shaped myself to fit it. Reactionary politics, chauvinism, institutional religion ... the list could go on. And I suppose I still believe in protest, but more out of tribal loyalty than anything. Sometimes all of those things feel like expressions of the suffocation I can't seem to escape rather than impressions of a culture I want to condemn.

'I'm a sucker for causes. I can never think of a cause myself. I mean, left to my own imagination, I would never have come up with something like vegetarianism or equal rights for women. It just wouldn't happen. So, instead, I have always managed to feel angry about other people's causes. They satisfy my need to punch things. But I suppose protest can never settle on anything. Let's face facts; it can't even settle on a husband."

She threw the olive at me again. This time it glanced off my ear.

I thought about when she had said. Then I looked at the dog.

"This dog," I said, pointing at the dog, "he belongs to someone called Lanier."

The dog stayed in the same position, stretched out on the floor, his head lying on his front paws.

"Come again?"

"Look at his collar. It says that he belongs to someone called Lanier who lives on the Rue d'Amsterdam."

"Lanier?"

"That's right."

"You mean like your character in the ..."

"... in the film. Yes."

Alice turned to look at the dog. The dog's head stayed fixed to the floor, but his innocent eyes switched between us.

"So he belongs to ... I see."

"Do you see?"

"No."

"No."

"Lanier ..."

"But all of it ..."

"... all of what?"

"The film ... Rémy .... the dog. Like you, all of it makes me think."

She looked at the dog.

"What does it make you think?"

"Have you listened much to Caterina Valente?" I asked.

"No."

"She was born in Paris. I remember one time I was driving home from work, and a song came on the radio. It was a great song. I had never heard it before. It was by Caterina Valente and it was called La golondrina. I think it means 'The swallow', but beyond that I don't speak … so I mean I didn't know what it was all about, really. Even so, it was a beautiful song. But as I was driving along and this song was playing, three things happened quickly: one, a car pulled out from a parking space and nearly crashed into me; it beeped at me, and I could see the driver making … well, gestures. Two, an ambulance came screaming by me from behind, and I had to pull over onto the curb. And finally, a woman pushed a young man, who I assumed was her boyfriend, from the pavement out into the middle of the road so that I nearly ran him over. They were obviously having an argument because she was shouting at him, like you wouldn't believe. She was a large women and not someone I would want to get on the wrong side of, if you know what I mean.

'And the combination of these three things left me feeling a little … anxious, not happy, not able to just relax as I drove. And it was only as I was pulling into my parking space that my attention turned back to the song. I remember feeling sorry, or some kind of regret, because even as the song was coming to a close, I could enjoy it free of distraction.

'I sat for a moment in my car, once the song had ended, and I had turned off the radio and the engine. I remember thinking that, for the last few minutes of my journey, the song had remained constant. It had always been there, but things had got in the way so that I couldn't hear it."

Alice threw another olive at me.

BY A RIVER

The light was beginning to go out of the day. We walked towards the final scene of our enactment more or less in silence, stopping only to pass comment on the sunset or to check the time. The silence had crept up around us, almost unnoticed, the closer we had come to understand the origins and character of our shared memory. It was curious. For the last two days Alice could scarcely keep her mouth shut, and, quiet though I had been, I had wanted to keep the conversation going. From one perspective, everything that had happened made any conversation look futile. If we had words to say to each other, they were waiting for us down by the river.

Not that it was uncomfortable. In some ways, just the opposite. I felt relaxed as we made our way to meet with Rémy, and I intuited something similar from Alice. To walk with my new friend – if that's what she was – in a mood of quiet calm, after we had, apparently, reached as close to the end of our search for the impenetrable memory as we could, was settling. For the first time, uninterrupted by our problem, we became oblique figures in a painting of Parisian life, nestled into the charm of the city. I noticed things in a way that I had noticed them when I had wandered around on my own. And I thought about the things I noticed.

I noticed a very fat man staggering about in a clumsy and unkempt way on a boat moored to the bank of the river. He could have been drunk, but I wasn't sure. He thrashed around for something, but once-removed from clear sight of what it was. He stopped in his tracks. Then, a little urgently, he muttered something under his breath, and rushed to the side of the barge, where he vomited into the water. I don't know what he had been eating, but his vomit was flecked with emerald green, and came out of him like an endless mass of unwrapped sausage meat.

I tried to walk by in a nonchalant fashion, but couldn't help, in the spirit of Rémy's metaphysical speculation, think about what this might signify. Just as the memory was threading things together from a wider angle to say something to us that we would otherwise not notice, was this fat man tincturing the surface of the Seine with half-digested cabbage soup as a not-so-subtle comment on the frivolity with which I graced the cobblestones of the great city?

"Huurgh," said the man one more time.

I tried to look in the other direction.

"A heavy lunch?" Alice wondered out loud.

"Perhaps," I said.

The woman in front of us was walking a dog on a lead. I could only see it from behind. Our dog was at my side, hanging around my ankles. The creature in front of us was smaller, well-groomed and chic. It was the sort of dog that might have been ordered from a boutique and shipped to the owner in precise but minimalist wrapping. I probably could, in my head, hold a conversation with it, but did I really want to? I thought I would probably come out the other side feeling somehow coarse and wanting in taste. And the way the dog moved made me think that any conversation would be acerbic and pointed, with no more than one or two sharp but well-chosen words, intended as much to repel as engage.

So instead I talked to the dog at my side. This kept me amused for a good two-thirds of the time it took us to reach the bench just beyond the Pont des Arts.

"Is it me, or are you holding back?" I would ask the dog.

"What do you mean?"

I gestured at the dog trotting – or pattering – along ahead of us.

"Oh ... I see ... no ... the smell ... no ... it's all wrong. Best to steer clear, if you know what I mean."

"Different class?"

"Not the sort that will let any old nose poke around its posterior, I'm afraid. Precious. A little precious; that's how I would put it."

"I know the sort."

"Oh yes?"

"Absolutely. More people are precious about their posterior than you might think."

"I don't understand it. Call me crazy, but if you want to

smell my arse, you can smell my arse."

I credited the dog's pragmatic philosophy.

"Precious," the dog repeated, "that's what it is."

"So you're more of an open book?" I said.

"I don't know about that. But I like to think I have a friendly disposition. Start from the assumption that most creatures are basically all right. That's how I like to work it. Maybe there are one or two exceptions. Maybe every now and then you get your nose burnt. Maybe every now and then someone hoses you off the street. Maybe every now and then a vagrant aims his boot at your backside. Maybe every now and then you find yourself without a proper home to go to or someone charitable enough to brush a few crumbs of salmon en croute from their table in your general direction. But what can you do? Life can't be crumbs of salmon en croute for everyone."

"You have a plucky frame of mind."

"I mean it's quite galling when you see one's like her," the dog said, referring to the dog ahead of us. "All fluff and flounce, lording it over you when their good fortune is just that: the flighty fancy of fortune. I mean to say, sometimes it doesn't seem right, you know; that I'm down here slumming it in the gutter, fighting over a few scraps of mouldy bread while she ... or all the ones like her ... are up there, living life literally in the lap of fortune. One day it might be nice to get an affectionate tickle behind the ear, or a nuzzle in heavily perfumed hair.

'But I'm not complaining, you understand. Life's good. I'm philosophical about it."

I thought for a moment.

"Can I ask you something?" I asked.

"Of course," said the dog.

"I mentioned it before. This weekend the lady at my side and I have been caught up in something quite strange. We can both remember scenes from a story, but we don't know how we have come to remember them. That's where we are going now. We are on our way to act out the final scene. At this point in time, I have no idea what the scene comprises and what we will say, but when it comes to it – when the scene actually begins, I mean – the words will just pour out of me. It will go off like clockwork. I don't know what it is, but in the same way that I know I will know what to say, my hunch is that you have something to do with all this. You are somehow part of this 'thing' - if that's what it is – that we are remembering. What have you got to say to that?"

"Sounds pretty farfetched to me," said the dog.

"Yes. I suppose so."

"In fact, if I weren't a talking dog in the imagination of a young man with nothing better to do, I'd call it a silly thing."

"Yes."

"As silly as a song," said the dog.

"Oh?" I replied.

In the same way as before, I drifted back into silence, very much aware that there was no conversation, and in particular that we were not so anxiously fixated on the remembrance that had troubled us all weekend. This second return to silence made my mind want to lay claim to it, to seek tuition under it so that it might, through some impossible transmission of vacant air and sound, enlarge my understanding.

Monks understood this kind of thing, I thought. A few years ago I had visited the recreated ruins of a Carthusian monastery. The life it suggested was, in its own way, quite appealing. Each monk lived in, not so much a cell, as a small wooden cottage, with a garden to tend, untroubled by the obligation to engage anyone in conversation. Even as a tourist I found it strangely peaceful and compelling. My imagination, acting on the circumstance, or a memory guilded in the fallen stones, had worked to make itself known. I remember I walked around quietly content for some time afterwards.

My visit to the Carthusian monastery, and perhaps the visits of all its tourists, contained a paradox. How can a place that cultivates silence in such seclusion, and which after four hundred years is nothing more than a ruin, still impress a sense of identity with such force? How can something that has turned self-denial and self-overcoming into its guiding principle cultivate such a strong personality? Why was it not destroyed and forgotten by the bull in history's china shop? It was not simply that this place had managed to cling to a withered and battered remnant of itself; on the contrary, it had an identity and power that was almost unique. How, I thought again, is it possible to find this sort of 'noise' among so much silence?

My mind began to wander in another direction. How would life as a Carthusian monk work in practice? In the refectory, for example, it must have been frustrating to have to point at things rather than simply ask for them. How much easier it would have been to say "Please pass me the salted fish", rather than point and receive the salad vegetables instead. I supposed it didn't work like this; no doubt there were ways and means; no doubt there were simple codified gestures substituted for speaking. Even so, I could easily imagine the depths of aggravation to which this kind of life might drive me on days when no form of communication really worked. Suppose you had asked the Sacrist for a book and he gave you the wrong one; suppose you then spent several hours rubricating a dry and monotonous tome about fungus; suppose you then went out to work in the gardens and every time you wanted one of your brethren to help you shift some earth, they just passed you a shovel; and suppose you then went to the refectory, pointed at the salted fish and received the salad vegetables. Supposing this, I think I might have been tempted, at this point, to stand up and shout "Just pass me the fucking salted fish!"

And then I wondered what if, in deference to an unusual world-wide craze, everyone decided to renounce speech, and go about their daily lives pointing at things, or, in rare moments of self-indulgence, grunting. Would things be better or worse? Intuitively, you would think that everything in the external world would quickly become anonymous or lose the forensic definition that words confer on them. But, perhaps a little willfully, I was not entirely sure; just as words can be used to perfume and adorn relationships, more often than not they can poison and induce a rancorous stink. How many long-term married couples might, I wondered, deep down feel some twinge of relief at the mere thought of a relationship sustained but with the words taken out?

And what about the awkward 'social etiquette' of chatting up, the sort of winning exchanges and cocksure conquests that grease the gear stick of twentysomething flings? Imagine these exchanges with the words subtracted and there is no great appreciable difference, and even some human dignity salvaged: man looks at woman; woman looks with distant but available amusement at man; man nods and points at rows of luminous vodka; woman shrugs shoulders and smiles; man smiles, looks pleased with himself and nods inquiringly at woman's boobs; woman shrugs shoulders and remains available. Barroom romance is hardly the eloquent and chivalrous entreaties of courtly love.

So, I thought, in the absence of words, how and where exactly is the deficit, and is there not a craftily coined revenue? Was this furtive trick something that institutionalised Christianity had made its own centuries ago and something we have since forgotten? Are words a weak and unwarranted attempt to make the world fit an anthropocentric mould, an attempt that it effortlessly and derisively resists? And if the attempt were relinquished would things, in this Carthusian silence, crystallise as they really are? I wondered.

The silence between Alice and I could, of course, be explained by the fact that we had already said so much to each other. We had just come to the end of the words that were available in the crowded time and space we had shared for the last two days. We were, even if only unconsciously, taking a break.

But, my bent of mind and the broad line of the events we had followed, meant that there was another way to look at it. This was not exhaustion or the dead end of our combined imagination; this was the influence of the memory. We were gradually resigning to the lilt and lyric of the words in our head. We had outsourced our conversation.

Were these characters, into whose roles we had stepped, abstractions waiting to steal the form of an unwitting host? Were they cheating us of our own matter? Or was there a more positive way to look at it? Was it, in fact, a better way for the two of us to hold a conversation? Did it provide a channel to mediate something otherwise peripheral or even unknown? In more ways than one, there was something ghostly about these performances. They worked their charm through our close proximity and a simple combination of human elements.

We saw Rémy waiting on the bench. His legs were stretched out and his head hung forward, like he was inspecting his shoes. As we drew near, he must have caught sight of us. He turned, and leaned back on the bench, resting one arm on the seat to support the weight of his upper body.

"Well," he said, once we had come to rest in front of him, "we meet again."

"So to speak."

He smiled.

"I was just reflecting. I was trying to observe the point at which all of this might seem like a deja vu. Would it come to me as I stared at the river? Or would it arrive with you? Or would it, no matter how well prepared I might be, surprise me."

"And has 'it' arrived?"

"You will know better than me. But I would say no. What would you say?"

"I would agree."

"But, all the same, something is lingering about us."

I took that to be a smell of urine, but truth is often subjective.

"So you have had the afternoon together and you have thought about everything I told you this morning? You have cogitated, shall we say?"

"We have cogitated."

We sat down next to him. I sniffed warily at the scented air.

"So what can you tell us?" she asked.

The mere thought of this last scene was more welcoming than bumbling about the concourse of the Gare de Lyons. It was, on the face of it, much simpler: two people seated on the banks of the river, along the Palais des Tuileries. Compared with the exposure and emotional turbulence of the day before, this was a holiday within the holiday my long weekend was meant to be.

Some of the details from this scene we knew from the letter Rémy had read to us; but he filled out the picture. It was to begin by mirroring the first scene: the countess was sitting alone on a bench, staring forlornly into the currents of the river, when the watchmaker catches sight of her in the distance from the bridge. The river setting and the mood of the countess, while not in any way made explicit, were to suggest the possibility – the visual thought – of suicide. The watchmaker, we were to understand, is frightened by what he sees, which enlivens his approach. We were also to understand that something like a few months had elapsed between the last scene and this one.

Once we were settled and ready to begin, I turned to walk – pointlessly – back up to the bridge. Alice took me by the arm.

"You don't need to walk up to the bridge."

"It helps to set the scene," I said.

Now that we had gone to all this trouble, it seemed petty and feeble not to do it properly.

As I climbed the steps back up the bridge, I could feel a stirring of adrenalin give new life to my thoughts and movements.

I walked a little way, then stopped. I looked down at Alice, uncertain if I would be able to detect at what point exactly the scene would begin. I thought she might give me a signal: a wave, or a nod of the head. But she kept the same position; she crossed her arms across her stomach, and leaned forward, swaying enough to suggest the wind had the power to make her move. Rémy lingered in the background, offset from the bench, propping his back against the wall. I could see him looking towards me.

The thought on which he had dwelled when we first saw him was infectious. The scene was obviously meant to begin with me, but how would I know when to start it? Would I just decide, or would something come to me? And if something just came to me, would I then know everything I was about to say? Or would I have to wait? If I tried to analyse it in this fashion, what had happened, and what was about to happen, resisted. It was clearly there waiting for me. It was real. But I couldn't make it accountable.

I knew the memory existed, and I knew the scene would take place just as the last two scenes had run their course smoothly. I knew this, not because of the precedent, but because I was not worried. If I had been acting out a scene that relied on words I had tried to memorise and practise, I would be nervous; I would be frightened that I would forget, fail to enunciate, mumble. But because my efforts were not required, I could let the memory take over. I could trust it. And I had the strong sense that, if I spent all my time at this point concentrating hard to pinpoint when the scene should start, it would never begin, and I would remain rooted to the bridge willing this cycle of insanity into existence.

I began the return walk to the bench. As I walked, I realised that the decision to start walking must have come while I was day-dreaming, as though someone had pushed a button to make my legs start moving while my mind was elsewhere. Fleetingly, I wondered if that was the explanation. If I could halt my mind, if I could erase it from the moment, would I then begin to see what was actually taking place? But it also struck me that this was a little like trying to understand decapitation by cutting off my head. So I didn't labour the thought.

I approached Alice. I stopped a few metres away. The dog was rummaging about behind the bench. Then it ran round, sniffed at her ankles, and looked at me inquisitively. My mind was unsure of itself. I took the final few steps. The dog barked at me. I stopped walking.

WATCHMAKER
What are you doing?

COUNTESS
Oh ... nothing.

WATCHMAKER
But I mean ...

COUNTESS
Nothing. I'm doing nothing, Lanier.

The dog barked at me again.

WATCHMAKER
With Charlemagne. What are you doing with Charlemagne?

COUNTESS
Charlemagne?

WATCHMAKER
My dog. My dog, Charlemagne, yes? What are you doing?

The dog barked again.

COUNTESS
Your dog?

WATCHMAKER
My dog.

COUNTESS
I didn't know he was your dog.

WATCHMAKER
Well, he is my dog. Charlemagne, come on boy!

The dog trotted up to me, and I tickled him behind the ear.

COUNTESS
I didn't know you had a dog.

WATCHMAKER
Yes. [To Charlemagne] Where have you been boy? Where have you ... why did you wander off like that? You never do that. Didn't you know I missed you?

I suddenly felt sad. I sat down on the bench next to Alice. The dog followed me. Tears came to my eyes.

WATCHMAKER
I thought you had … gone. I thought you had gone. But you're all right! Thank God you're all right, my boy!

Once again the dog barked. Then licked my hand.

COUNTESS
I see you're close.

WATCHMAKER
You could say that.

COUNTESS
He's been following me around. Charlemagne.

WATCHMAKER
You? He's been following you?

COUNTESS
Yes

WATCHMAKER
Since when?

COUNTESS
Since when? Now let me see, I'd say since around the time we first met. Give or take a day or two.

WATCHMAKER
Really?

COUNTESS
I gave him one or two scraps. He came back. Strange, don't you think?

I looked at the dog.

WATCHMAKER
He ran away to you.

COUNTESS
I'm not sure I'd put it quite like that!

WATCHMAKER
No, no, that's exactly how it is. He ran away to you.

COUNTESS
Well, even if he did, he's come back to you now.

I thought about this.

WATCHMAKER
What are you doing here? Like this.

COUNTESS
You don't like this place, then?

WATCHMAKER
I ... I saw you from the bridge ... I saw Charlemagne.

COUNTESS
And you thought you might join me.

WATCHMAKER
In this location ... you looked ...

COUNTESS
Unless, of course, that too was a pretence.

WATCHMAKER
Whatever harsh things I may have said, I would not ... I wish you no harm.

COUNTESS
I pretended to be someone else – no it's not over yet – I am pretending to be someone else.

WATCHMAKER
You told me.

COUNTESS
But I couldn't ensnare you.

WATCHMAKER
Why should I let you? You tell a lie like that, where does it stop?

COUNTESS

It isn't a scientific principle, Lanier. People tell lies for reasons. Surely the lie is weighed in the strength of the reason.

WATCHMAKER

That's one way of looking at it.

COUNTESS

But not one you credit?

WATCHMAKER

You tell me you are not who you said you were. You admit that you were trying to manipulate me, but you won't tell me who you really are or the reason for your manipulation. How can I weigh a reason when I don't know what it is? And why should I take your word for it? That – surely – is not unreasonable?

COUNTESS

Then it's your reason pitted against mine.

WATCHMAKER

I would not base anything on that kind of blind faith.

COUNTESS

I want to convince you in a different way.

WATCHMAKER
By not telling me the truth?

COUNTESS
You have a … you are a brutal man.

WATCHMAKER
True or false. That's straight-forward enough isn't it?

COUNTESS
I did lie to you. I've said so already. I'm not who I said I was. You only know the counterfeit. But circumstances – and you must realise that for some of us these are difficult times – mean that it would be imprudent, perhaps even dangerous, for me to reveal my real identity. I had hoped – or I had come to hope … So no … you see, no … I don't agree …

Alice broke off. I thought, at first, that she was about to cough or something was caught in her throat, but when I looked at her, I could see that she was thinking; her eyes fluttered over the cross-currents of the river and the shifting human scenery about it. Finally, she looked briefly, and with a hint of amusement, at me.

She didn't say anything, and without further delay, returned to our words. But this strange hiatus affected me, and I found myself staring at her as she spoke the next lines. I thought about why she had paused, and at once I felt confident, if not sure, of the answer. Her pause was a response to the lines she had been speaking, and suggested their relevance to us. I inched sluggishly towards a further thought: just as the countess was looking for a fake identity in which to recover a stable form of life, and with it love, so we were wearing costumes through which we might come together. Alice's little look of amused pleasure intimated this moment of love by proxy.

My mind was racing.

COUNTESS
I say 'I had come to hope' ... at first I only wanted to ... I just wanted to escape ... and I would have done anything.

WATCHMAKER
But then you looked in my eyes ...

COUNTESS
Don't you see? ... I mean, if you think like that no wonder you ... disguises don't have to be deceptions. The more time I spend doing this – 'deceiving' you and others about who I am – the more I feel naked without the disguise. Like there is a screen, and it stands between me and everything – I mean everything – around me. That's why I am staring at the river. That's where your cynicism leads.

Something had dropped from Alice's voice. It was difficult to say what exactly. Where she had, in every previous scene, delivered the words in a way that would only serve the character she was playing, these last words seemed to give her own personality more room. While she was not speaking as Alice, she was, in some sense, more obviously present in the words.

COUNTESS
And it is only in what I say, tainted with all its disguises and falsehoods, that you will ever find anything. If you will not put your arms around this marionette, then, in different ways, the elements will sweep us away.

Alice wavered again. She repeated the last few lines. This time she spoke slower, savouring – or interpreting – their meaning.

COUNTESS
... If you will not put your arms around this marionette, then, in different ways, the elements will sweep us away.

I shot her a look that must have been caught between curiosity and empathy. I reached out to place a hand on her arm. I was on the point of saying something but could not find what I wanted to say. 'Are you all right, Alice?' was an obvious question, but in the mood her utterances had created, any break from the scene felt like it would disturb the spell of its words. So, after an uncertain pause, I continued.

WATCHMAKER
This is an unusual reckoning.

COUNTESS
Yes.

I – the watchmaker – reflected on the Countess' remarks.

WATCHMAKER
When you first met me, you might remember that I was a little subdued because I had lost my only friend. My only friend was this dog, the most loyal and lovable creature I have known. But in the time I got to know you, I came to think that perhaps he was right to leave me. I am a cold man. Withdrawn. Misanthropic even. Who would want to keep company with someone like that?

But now I see him here with you ... I would trust this dog above anyone or anything. And I believe that he has led me to you. He is trying to tell me something. Now that I think about it, I would say that he trying to lead me towards a better kind of life. A better kind of living.

COUNTESS
I am more sincere in my affections than you want to believe.

WATCHMAKER
Yes. I know.

Our rehearsed words, at this moment, became rehearsed movements. Instinctively, we both knew what to do. The countess lowered her head. I leaned forward to embrace her.

The dog settled in a ball at our feet.

OPPOSITION

I couldn't say when exactly it happened, but Alice was holding my hand. It was dark, and we hid in the shadows that crept, like damned creatures, from the river. The sound of traffic remained and was more noticeable now that we had stopped talking. Rémy had wandered away from us and was sitting on the river bank, his legs dangling over the edge.

We all now occupied the same moment of silence. Including the dog, who was lying asleep in front of us. The quiet mood that surrounded us somehow complemented the scene that had preceded it. We had all surrendered to the memory, and it left us satisfied and sleepy.

I had sensed all this before the scene took place. I had known that nothing I could have said apart from the words we were speaking would do anything other than disjoin the rhythm in the exchange. The unexpected silence from any voice outside the 'stage' circumscribed us, and was so intense it had almost snuffed us out of existence.

When I look back on it, Alice and I had receded into the

shadows. The 'Alice' I had known for a few days, and the 'I' I could refer to flippantly, seemed like a steady and unbroken reality. But the memory had gradually eroded it. In this last scene down by the river, the machinations of the memory were complete. We had conceded to our characters so willingly and naturally that, through them, 'Alice and I' became a reflection on the surface of a lake that might disappear with the slightest ripple.

The story led the way: the countess snared her man, not by revealing her true identity, but by asking the watchmaker to love the disguise she had created. The implication of this for any observer was clear: that its disguises were the only immediate form in which anything of any importance or value might come to light.

These moments with Alice, in the course of my long weekend, were the strangest and hardest to grasp, because our situation did not settle in any one direction. We had, to be sure, found time for each other over the weekend, and I enjoyed her company. But our transformation into characters who appeared to have somersaulted into 'love' was oddly jarring; we had become the sport and its spectator, and, as spectators, weirdly mesmerised by the sport.

Some of this I grasped faintly in the moment, but I didn't really have time to reflect; and yet part of what was happening in our dialogue was an open invitation to reflect. The more I think about it, the more I am convinced that this was the aim of Rémy's story. He wanted – or the story wanted – the two people to embrace it while recognising that they were only playing a part. This was tacit at the very least in his own letters, reflections on memory, and the purported aim of recreating the cinematic world of Lucienne De Metz. Everything in the story, ourselves included, was most real when it was unmasked as a conjuring trick.

"Okay, that's enough of that," Alice had said after the dog had appeared and then settled comfortably at our feet.

Her voice had been tearful.

"All this nonsense," she had said.

I found that, in the rising dark, I could fix my eyes on any one object and, with no conscious effort, let my brain play with it. I could just make out the shape of trees on the other bank. Lingering on them, barely discernible branches and leaves became, at first, wisps of hair on a head sweeping skywards, responding, perhaps, to a current of electricity in the climate; and then, over each tree, I managed to create formless patches and shapes, the lineaments of eyes and mouths with doll-like smiles.

I cleared this mirage with a blink and waited for whatever came next. The shape of the trees faded into blackness, and then the scene jumped, in the way that a film from an old projection reel might jump; and pursuing this blip, my eyes began to read in the patch of land across the river, dots that joined into scarcely intelligible letters and incomplete words with different possible meanings.

The dog twitched as it lay before us, on the very edge of the embankment.

I caught fragments of conversations as people walked by. These were mostly in French, but sometimes I thought I could detect a foreign tongue: Spanish, something Asiatic,

American. Whether I heard the words or not, I never heard enough to grasp the full meaning. I overheard the occasional trill of French loaded with enough meaning to raise my attention, but enough lack of clarity to invite mental mischief. My interpretation of these conversations was a pagan God crudely conjoined from the material parts of man and beast, or some other fantasy welded together from a simple encounter with material things. The words 'chicken', 'garlic' and 'death' came to my ears via a smart-looking young couple. I imagined them walking naked down a candlelit corridor wearing chains of garlic and brandishing dead chickens in performance of a necromantic rite considered edgy and subversive in metropolitan Parisian society. These media types, I thought.

Two American girls stepped with a scowl around the dog. They mentioned the word 'monkey' more than once, and as I zoned in and out of eavesdropping, also seemed to be talking about Italian ice cream. The connection was hard to make; unless of course they had recently been to Italy and, on one day out, spent the afternoon eating ice cream as they walked around the monkey enclosure of a zoo. This, to my reckoning, didn't admit much possibility; so I began to wonder if 'monkey' was just a name given to an exotic flavour of ice cream. And then I imagined the two girls strolling along by the Seine eating cornettoes of vanilla ice cream studded with monkey eyeballs and decorative shavings of hair, decrying mint choc chip as uncultivated and coarse.

Alice sighed and wrapped her arm inside mine.

I stopped to let these thoughts catch the current of the river, and watched them disappear downstream. They, of all things, would not 'admit much possibility'; they only made any kind of sense as thoughts. In the company of another person, familiar or unfamiliar, they would flounder, weaken and reveal a person descending into the abyss of an unregulated mind. To reflect, muse, mull, was a withdrawal. My mind, unable to claw its fingernails into any sweating flesh, found no purchase over anything, and could only wander further and further afield.

To sit and watch people in the city of Paris – or simply to watch the city itself – goaded its romantic stereotype, so that it took flight on this wayward imagination. But, just like the cryptic fragments of meaning on which I could eavesdrop, or the distorting perspective I could find simply by staring at the same cluster of objects for a length of time, conscripting the city inwards stole it from the world of people and things. It turned it into something more rarefied, less complete and determinate, a 'place' without place.

And in doing this, it took me back to my starting point: a tourist cut off from the city of romance because I was a tourist, and not part of the culture. When I had stepped off the train for the first time and into the city, I remember that I did not feel daunted, or any inclination to seek out a café or bar and strike up a conversation. The experience of being a foreigner cut off from the ordinariness of everything surrounding was a concentrated form of the drug for which I had already found a liking. This situation confounded the opportunity to collapse the boundaries at every turn: in a café or a shop, I could not make pleasant chit-chat; in parks and public places, friendly strangers found me as human and engaging as any one of the trees.

For much of the time, my mind associates with its body more through custom and nicety than consent; and when their combined existence collides with another it can sometimes feel like I am witness to an out-of-body experience. On the night I arrived in Paris, and as I was making my way to my hotel, a man approached me from across the street. He was middle-aged; he had an uneven beard veneered with grime, and the hard surface of his skin gave it the texture of treated metal. He spoke to me in a deep voice. I said I was sorry, that I was English, and that I could not understand everything he was saying. He begrudged an acknowledgement, but continued to speak, mainly in French, with the occasional word rendered into something like English.

Our conversation continued for a while until it withered into nothing. But, after I had absorbed the initial shock of speaking to a stranger, I managed to find a comfortable distance on the conversation. I soon stopped trying to understand what he was saying, and started thinking about the dishevelled state of his beard, which looked like it might have been offering shelter to lice; and from here I could imagine little lice, invisible in the dusk, climbing up to the tips of individual hairs in his beard, and then leaping aggressively at me in an expeditious bid to establish a new colony. From his beard, my study of the man roamed upwards towards his pate, which was bald and imprinted with the mark of sharp objects. I could picture the man with a sprig of barbed wire adding decoration to an otherwise empty site.

So, as I thought these things while I nodded my head and said the occasional, but hollow, word, I could more or less witness and document the extent of my distance from the matter and dimensions of the object with whom I was nominally engaged. In especially long conversations, it sometimes felt that my mind could go off for a five-minute stroll in the park, while my body completed the business of keeping up appearances.

With a mind that would not settle on anything, the thought of romance was no more grounded. It would simply not obey any bodily instinct. Any force that imparted life to material things, my mind would steal, and set free into thinness of air.

The dog was still asleep. I watched it breathe deeply.

And then I thought about the other side of the coin. Alice was quite different.

If my mind was in a permanent state of withdrawal, Alice's was in a permanent state of conquest. Even where the odds were stacked against her – or perhaps especially so – she wanted to wrestle with a situation or a person until it suited the shape she wanted to give it.

Alice took Paris and channelled it through her being. Her Paris was a place to celebrate the breakdown of a reactionary world-order, of men in uniforms declaiming loudly an inflexible code of conduct. Romance in the city, for Alice, coincided with the voices of political and social alienation, the charismatic, sometimes subversive, ways they found to think and conduct themselves in public. And Alice's world was so sexually liberated that it lived in a state of constant physical exhaustion.

In every respect, by outward appearance, Alice was a statement in capital letters. And, at first glance, it was hard to imagine how anyone might share in her world, except where they agreed to its every particular. She did not seem to give things space, to allow them to settle into their own distinctive shape. She wanted, by instinct, to turn them, challenge them, reform them. Left to itself, life was a fossilising relic of prehistory; it needed the impetus and vitality of change and discovery to imbue it with spirit and force, so that it might become truly meaningful.

This was, as I had discovered, by no means the complete picture; if there had been nothing more to Alice than this, then I am sure we could not have found time for each other. I even thought that her state of possessive protest was, archetypally, the precondition for my withdrawal.

I thought about what would have happened if Alice and I had met at the same age. If we had both met when we were young, we would not have forged the same connection. The mature Alice was intimidating enough, but a post-adolescent version with principles, tearing chunks out of the Neanderthal objects in her way, was a frightening thought. This strain of high fervour was a potential death trap for any clueless young man. Any connection at that age would have been approximate to mathematical impossibility. At every turn, or in response to every move the young Alice might make, I suspect that I would have found a discreet way to avoid her. But the young Alice in my head was too strident and radical to find much interest in an unreactive robot like me.

If, on the other hand, we had both met in maturity, again the chemistry would not have worked. The future me was reclusive, but stubbornly so, and less tolerant of a scratched and broken counter-cultural record. If I thought about a middle-aged version of myself with a quiet life in a small urban flat, hemmed in by books and unmarked boxes of clutter, scowling at the way people drive impatiently, I could feel a glimmer of irritation at Alice. And Alice, in return, would sneer at my fussy attitude and pre-liberal existence by telling me about all the men in front of which she had masturbated, and the sense of release and liberation this had occasioned.

So, as peers, we had little hope; but the age gap – the younger me versus the older Alice – created possibilities where the narrow conventions of one generation would close them down. Alice the conqueror went looking for un-moulded matter in my quietness; but turned strangely mellow in its company, reverting to the teenage romantic she had always wanted to be.

She rested her head on my shoulder.

It was this silhouette of absolute monarchy in the path of anarchy that interested me about her, and had interested me since we first met in the Jardin des Plantes. The naivety she had watched recede with her twenties was the character she wanted to recover; and the more time we had spent together, the more I thought I could detect this girl with a head full of cinematic sentimentalism. And the more the character took shape, the more I found that I wanted to share in her sentimentalism.

Inevitably, the narrow space of a long weekend would not allow me to see a fuller picture of her. Had I met her in the middle of a crisis? Or was this internal contradiction a crack that ran deep through the grain of her life? Either way, in the hours I had spent with her, I had witnessed the assembling and disassembling of her personality, the latter following hard upon the former.

In different ways, then, and in ways that seemed to take root and grow independently, we were the basket cases of romance: I had a mind incapable of associating with any object, and Alice had a mind that wanted to possess objects to a degree that caused their – and her own – destruction. But both of us, in the company of each other and with the charge of a city willing the invention and reinvention of love, intuited something we could not describe or represent in any accurate or sensible form.

So we were, from different shades of deficiency, short of words to bridge the gap between us; and it was clear, looking back on the last few days, that the words lodged in our heads made up for this shortage. Rémy's story was an artificial limb to replace an amputation; it fulfilled a role; it supplied the missing words without which we looked like blanched tourists walking into the middle of the road with our noses in a map scrawled upon by tourist-information officers.

The strangest part was to participate by standing in the

locations described on the page and speaking the words, while one part of my brain stood in the audience watching all this happen. But 'strange' does not entirely do justice to it. Looking outside-in on our little piece of theatre, it was, in lots of ways, farcical. Most obviously, we were simply very bad actors. The wet trousers, tears and simmering sense of anarchy in primary school productions were more compelling and dramatically poignant than our feeble renditions. And even the most aesthetically purblind and incompetent director would not have cast us in the roles. Why? Because we obviously looked like misfits; we were different ages, different temperaments, different people entirely. Only in a pantomime version of the film that enjoyed watching men with big beards play women with big boobs would we have ever been cast. This was the right analogy; we were, so to speak, men with beards playing women to the lowest standards in physical comedy.

I watched the dog breathe. The movement of its rib cage was measured and precise. It had curled its head comfortably into its body, and even its tail had coiled inwards towards a core that pulled from the inside.

It must be nice, I thought, to be able to fall asleep in the middle of a city, indifferent to the inconvenience it might cause. And it was just as impressive that the dog could fall asleep so soon after joining our company. In human terms this was a little like a guest coming over for dinner, handing over their coat, going through the bare minimum of social pleasantries, and then falling asleep on the carpet. If the analogy were extended, the guest would probably only wake up long enough to relieve themselves on a pot plant before they left.

I wondered, once again, where this dog had come from.

The dog began to breathe rapidly, and we could hear muted barking in its sleep, no doubt caused by a happy figment of its imagination.

I could not say when exactly it happened, but at some point I put my arm around Alice.

Monday

A LETTER

My train was at midday, and I had to be out of the hotel, so I managed to clamber out of bed early. My first movements suggested I was either late or in a hurry. I remember staggering around my room, stumbling into the shower, cramming everything into my bag, and then checking under the bed several times to make sure I hadn't forgotten anything. I closed all the windows, swept through the bathroom, and checked the cupboards and the bed once again. But, as soon as I was ready, I sat down in the armchair where I had fallen asleep a couple of days before with the sight of Alice resting peacefully through the corner of my eye. I stayed in this position; for how long, I wasn't sure exactly, but it must have been at least five minutes.

The light from the window touched my face. I leaned forward slightly. My arms coiled into my body a little. The position made me look anxious. I looked up towards the window, and could just make out a few rooftops. My bag rested clumsily on the end of the bed. The speed and lack of care with which I had packed it meant that it now had the shape of a damaged potato. I could hear the noises of the city, but, from first impressions, it was quiet, almost serene.

I got ahead of myself. I went at speed through my walk to the station, the coffee I would drink before I left, the train to London and the coffee I would drink when I arrived. Then there would be the next journey: the journey home. I pictured my flat, my car, my journey to the office the next day. Even at this distance, I could sense their familiarity, and, although being in Paris made it seem otherwise, I knew I would fall back into my routines with no sense that I had been away, so that visiting Paris for a long weekend might seem, in retrospect, like an imaginary, rather than real, experience.

Already whenever I thought about the journey and what lay beyond it, a jolt of fear, noted with nausea, ran through my gut. My week ahead would be safe enough, but it would be unvaried, mechanical and unremarkable, surrounded by private hours of solitude and silence.

I soaked up the light of the morning sun on my face. I watched as its position changed slowly and a shadow receded down my arm, so that my skin could begin to feel the heat of daylight. The room was fairly tidy now that my sprawl was packed away; it bore a closer resemblance to a hotel room, simply because it did not look like it was inhabited. Looked at like this, even the room was willing me to vacate it. So I stood up and grabbed my bag.

I found a café. Something was on my mind. I fished out a notepad and pen from my bag. For a time I just sat, my coffee turning cold, unsure what to write.

Dear Alice,

I once heard a story about a man in middle age whose wife left him. This change led him to reflect on his life. I can't remember what he did for a living. It doesn't matter (or I think it doesn't ... sorry, I can't remember the exact details of the story). Anyway, he decided to quit his job, and escape his busy working life by going on a Buddhist retreat in Korea or somewhere in South East Asia. He spent a lot of time out there – several months at least – and said how calming and liberating he found it.

When he returned he said he struggled to tell people how real he thought the aspirations of Buddhist practice were. The simple meditative techniques, the peaceful and undisturbed routines, cut a clear path through the disorganised clutter and fickle attachments of his ordinary life. To step back and observe his mind and body, their habits and ingrained instincts, with no ground or sense of purpose that stood up to scrutiny, created, so he said, a sense of release, freedom and tranquillity.

He retained this feeling of tranquillity and calmness for a long time afterwards; and, as he resumed his life, he tried to make meditative practice a part of his routine. His whole experience also made him want to know more about Buddhism and Asian culture in general. So he read books on religion, history, philosophy, art and literature. He even began to study Sanskrit.

But as he returned to the familiarity of his old life, his memory and experience of retreat transformed with it. In particular, since his wife left him, he had not had any relationship with anyone; and while he had not been drawn to anyone throughout his retreat, he suddenly began to feel attracted to Asian women with an intense sexual desire he had not experienced since he was a teenager. He even had a fling with a Malaysian woman, but it fizzled out after only a few weeks. And, as it ended, he found that neither meditation nor his former interest in Asiatic culture carried with it the same appeal. They had burnt up through contact with material things. His interest lapsed altogether, and instead of calm and peaceful, he felt restless and subdued.

Is this a strange story to tell you? Even if it is, it is one that has stayed with me, and is, in my mind, related to the events of the last few days. I'm not sure how you should interpret it exactly. Like anything I suppose it might be interpreted in different ways. Was the 'calmness' that the man felt real? And, if so, why did it evaporate when he returned to his 'ordinary' life? Or might it all just look like a case of the 'grass is greener'. The quiet life of a Buddhist monk can seem especially appealing if you start from an uncomfortable place, but carried over a period of time, some of that 'calmness' might begin to wear thin. Then again a Nirvana that wears thin either gives the lie to the aspiration or is a dubious kind of Nirvana.

I don't know. As you can tell, as soon as I start thinking about something the less I am sure of anything and the more incoherent I become. But if – just suppose, even though you might not like it – the goals of the Buddhist life (or anything similar) are real, to my way of thinking, this story seems to say that how you do something matters. The arrangement and use of material things affects whether or not they return anything of any value. The form things take matters. And if the form is badly thought through, or, there is no form, then the goal for which you are striving can't possibly take shape. How could it?

Tomorrow my day-to-day life will resume. I will get up in the morning, make a coffee, eat breakfast, drive to work and studiously avoid talking to anyone for eight hours (unless I really have to). Then I will go home, have another coffee, read for an hour or more and try my hardest to sit in silence for the evening. Maybe I will go for a walk or watch a film. Something of this sort will then happen for the next three days. So runs the course of a modestly successful utility-maximising agent. And I don't want you to think that all of this happens against my will. Something about the contact that comes from my routine life makes me want to be alone.

And that's it. It's depressing and revealing enough that I can get to the bottom of my life as an adult human being in a single paragraph. It answers to nothing and no-one, and so must turn into nothing.

I hope it's clear what I'm saying: the 'form' of my life is badly thought through. It has no shape.

Yours
Sam

I tore the pages I had used out of the notepad. I folded the letter in half, and, with no clear intention, placed it in my jacket pocket. As I did this, I was not sure I would give the letter to Alice; and from this thought, I was dazzled into the prospect that I might not even see her again. We hadn't arranged to meet. But did that mean anything? I was sure I had told her the time my train left; not that I could remember her ever saying she would meet me at the station. The thought that I had seen the last of her had not really occurred to me.

I paid, slung my bag over my shoulder, and began the walk towards the station. It was not far away; no more than ten minutes. I found my way onto one of the main thoroughfares that supplied the station with traffic. The station's facade soon appeared in the distance.

Heaving my bag down the street, I thought about meeting her again; I chewed over what we might say to each other. In what sort of mood would I find her? With what caustic remark would she greet me? So far, her mood had always been transfigured by something from the day before. Still, to take the day before as the starting point for today was not that helpful, since it had ended more or less in silence; and most of the words we had spoken were not our own.

ON A STATION

At the front entrance, I checked my watch before I took in the spectacle of steel pillars scattered between the congress of humans and machines. I was early by an hour and a half, and drifted around the concourse, remembering my bearings and the practicalities of finding my train. This took no more than a minute or two.

It was a good view from the mezzanine. The vantage point meant I was sure I would spot Alice if she decided to say farewell. I tried to keep watch while I rummaged in my bag for my book, but my arms were not long enough, so I just leaned forward over the table and concentrated.

Light easily picked out holes in the station's structure, creating invasive shards that refracted in a conundrum of angles. People messed about on the concourse in different ways: some, either just naturally tense or panic-stricken, dodged around other people; others were obviously anxious but showed it by loitering around the same general area, checking the clock, loitering some more, checking the list of departures and then glancing with a frown at their watch. This last type were almost envious of the passengers who appeared to be genuinely worried and in a hurry; the need to worry, unfulfilled by any real reason, was itself the cause of worry. Still others moved with the grace of a mother bear imperceptibly attached to congeries of children.

Looking into the distance, I could just make out the spot where I had sat on the day I arrived. This was the seat on which I had sat facing the mother and her simian child. Thinking back to this moment, I tried hard to imagine myself sitting not opposite but next to her, with my arm around her shoulder as our child drifted dangerously towards the edge of our collective radar, and, at our call, returned to pester our attention. There would be imprecations and teasing within a unit of clumsy affection, relaxed by a lazy journey from one place to another. Picturing all of this was easy enough; I could catch my eye staring back at me; but I could not altogether remove the eye of the observer, so that I was totally immersed in the scene.

A loud bang erupted from somewhere towards the east end of the near distance. It sounded almost exactly like the bang I had heard the day before. Except this time, it was very clear that everyone had heard it. I could feel my eyes looking around hastily, seeking out the cause. One or two people around me had stood up and were peering over the balcony. As I got over the shock, and expected to find that something had fallen over, there had been an accident, or that the station had been attacked, I found that I couldn't. Those around me were the same: we simply couldn't see how the sound had come about. No obvious signs of destruction, disorder or disarray were visible. It didn't look like one of the pillars was about to come down. I picked out some of the station staff and traffic police, but even they looked mystified; they certainly weren't rushing towards an obvious site of emergency.

The striking thing about this loud noise was the effect. Stations at the height of the day are, self-evidently, noisy and convulsive places. This loud bang – which sounded like a sharp and thunderous diremption in the atmosphere – overwhelmed every other small fragment of noise and silenced them in an instant. Brief as it was, the moment of silence was extraordinary; but, by its nature, too extraordinary to really notice as it happened. In my case, I was already silent, but it burst through the noise in my head, smothering the possibility that I might open my mouth, or even move, in order to make a sound. The same thing, I assumed, had happened to everyone else. I had never before witnessed this sort of collective freeze. It suggested an imaginary perspective from which to witness everything and everyone in a level of detail that would have otherwise been lost in the constant flow of events. It tore a tiny hole through the combined consciousness of everyone on the station so that we all knew it had happened, but only after a beat of reflection. It was a moment that made you want to look over your shoulder.

A few shouts broke the silence, and a groundswell of general noise followed: people asking each other if they were all right, turning to someone nearby to see if they knew what had happened, or reaching for mobile phones. A hint of panic coursed through the station but nothing more. Since the staff were as clueless as everyone else, they obviously had no real idea how to reassure everyone. A few of them channelled their confusion through radios; others walked, full of authority but without purpose, through the open spaces between crowds of people.

Nothing else followed. No more bangs; the noise had not, so it seemed, foreshadowed something more grave and threatening. Jitteriness and caution checked the habits and movements of most people for a few minutes, but as things settled down, it was almost alarming how easily everyone returned to exactly what they were doing before the interruption.

Like everyone else, my first concern was to know what was going on, but when it became clear that no-one knew, and that this didn't matter, my thoughts tried to pick up where they had stopped; except they were now entangled in the disorder of what had happened.

The noise even tried to stir up other thoughts, as I began to forge my own unlikely analysis of its cause. It had, in a single disturbance, thrown everything up in the air. And this meant I couldn't think my way forward at all.

I looked around one last time, this time not expecting to see anything other than the station returning to its normal, undisturbed state. I looked across at the trains, and beyond them, to the tracks that led away from the city.

9 781838 127282

Printed by Libri Plureos GmbH in Hamburg,
Germany